MYL

SCHS –

from a 1975 graduate,

Mary Ridder

In Benton

MARY GUYNAN RIDDER

Dageforde Publishing, Inc.

ISBN 1-886225-71-0
Library of Congress Control Number: 2001097848
Cover design by Angie Johnson

Dageforde Publishing, Inc.
128 East 13th Street
Crete, NE 68333
Ph: (402) 826-2059 FAX: (402) 826-4059
email: info@dageforde.com

Visit our website: www.dageforde.com

Printed in the United States of America
10   9   8   7   6   5   4   3   2   1

To John, my grandfather;
Jack, my dad;
and John, my husband.
All men of the country.

Acknowledgments

My sincere appreciation to my editors and readers: your comments were appreciated more than you know.

Thank you, Phil Guynan, for listening and believing, and to my elementary teachers who not only placed dictionaries within my reach, but who also insisted that they be used.

To the farmers, ranchers, and small town champions across America: my thanks. You are my inspiration.

Every man is a volume
if you know how to read him.

—William Ellery Channing

1

Scraping in the dirt was helping. Getting dirt under my fingernails and stains in my jeans was forcing my mind to get down to earth. Some people take over companies for that thrill. Others beat their opponents in court for that "I won and you lost" high. Forget the people and their cases. Justice? Lord, no. This is about winning.

But lately, I've been digging in the dirt. My killer instinct is aimed at vanquishing those tormented portions of my brain and leaving everyone else to their own problems. Digging in soil is doing that for me. At the same time I'm getting dirty on the outside, my insides seem to be getting a lot cleaner.

That's how I came to find myself in Benton, Nebraska. The basic facts read like one of my client sheets: Thirty-something female with three dependents, if you count Ben. Ben is very independent, but at nine he still qualifies on my tax returns. Then there is Jane, seven, and five-year-old Tess.

We live in the Midwest in a town of fifteen hundred people surrounded by several thousand cows, rural vistas, and peace. Peace and quiet. Just what the doctor would have ordered, and exactly where I had to go if I was going to make it.

Exactly what I'm recovering from takes some untangling. Like Justin Melcher's kite in yesterday's sudden windstorm, I have some serious unraveling to do.

Oh, sure, I miss Minneapolis—the rush of a high-powered job, my friends and family. And I miss my marriage, or the one I thought I had.

But...I like Benton. It's the antithesis of what I was living before. Here you know who gossips and who doesn't, who's a public servant and who self-serves, and you share that big family feeling on a Friday night at the football field.

Of course I know all this simplicity is misleading; all people are complicated, all places have their problems, all of us have our own journeys to navigate. But you could do worse than Benton. I felt that the minute the kids and I arrived in my friend Annie's hometown.

ഉറ

"No matter how often I play, it comes out different each time," Liz said. "I've played the same hand over and over again. And then one day it hit me." Liz was pacing across Annie's sun porch. She paused, flicking a strand of hair from her dark brown eyes.

"I mean, I've played solitaire dozens of times on my computer. I'd click it on when I was waiting for a client to call me back or when I was bored with a project. And then one day I had this...this revelation."

She frowned at Annie and stepped into the living room. Throwing herself down on the leather sofa, Liz hugged a pillow and soaked in the sun's pulsating energy as it burst into their shared space. Little droplets of sun rays mixed with dust particles and sifted down to where she sat, struggling to explain.

Annie shifted on the opposite sofa. Across the road they could see the pastures cast orange as nightfall gathered in it's solitary thoughts.

"To think it takes a stupid simulated card game to help me understand. You know me, Annie. If it doesn't make sense to common sense Liz then it can't really be happening, right?"

Liz gave a thin slice of a laugh and angrily jerked her head, her throat burning from the bitter herbs she had swallowed over the past several months. Fighting for control, she drew her eyes back from the far corner of the sky and toward her friend.

"I'm glad I'm here," she ended.

Annie smiled the quick, sloppy smile Liz remembered from their first year in college. Her short, curly blonde hair bobbed when she nodded her head. "I'm glad you and your kids are staying with me. So, you want to work for my grandparents, do you?" she asked quietly, easing the mood. Annie never seemed to have a care in the world, but was always good at sensing when to move on.

"Well, I need a job and they need someone, right?" Liz answered simply, spreading her long fingers out in a basic gesture.

Looking back to the pasture, Liz quietly added, "I think it will be nice to just plant stuff. No heavy thinking, no impossible relationships. Just nice, simple landscaping jobs. One foot in front of the other." And then as if to herself, "I think I can handle that."

The sun sank lower, speeding now toward the horizon, sending thick shafts of multi-colored pinks, purples, and oranges across the evening sky. The cedar-paneled room was ablaze with light as it mirrored the sunset.

There was a loud commotion and the door flew open. In ran the Daniels gang with Ben in the lead. Jane was next with little Tess bringing up the rear. Laughter and some loud accusations followed with Liz doing very little refereeing. After letting them wind down, she ordered them to wash.

"And come back quieter, you hear me?" she shouted in the direction of the bathroom.

The three returned and joined Annie and their mom in the kitchen as they put together a salad and sandwich supper. More sibling banter, with several interpretations of the afternoon's explorations of a landscape still new to them, was served with the simple meal.

That night for what seemed like the hundredth time, Liz allowed herself to remember a little, relive some old hurts from her old life, feel some more of the pain. And then she closed her mind's door and slept the sleep people in the city assume people in the country always sleep."

ഔരു

Two weeks later Liz was a bonafide landscaper. At least the customers were satisfied. Spring fever had hit the area hard and her hands, expert or otherwise, were sorely needed. Droves of people, feeling that primitive earth pull, were anxiously deciding between cannas and hollyhocks, leaf or pine, and were coming to The Dirt Store to nurture their spring dreams.

Arch and Ruby Morrison had owned the small landscaping business in Benton for most of their married life. They'd met while working for the previous owner, courted while planting trees, shrubs, and flower groupings. They were married during the fall bulb season and had their five children during various planting or pruning seasons of the year. The store had served several surrounding communities for more than sixty years and was successful due to the Morrison's immense know-how, their work ethic, and their reputation for treating everyone the same.

They were now joined by granddaughter Annie's friend, the young woman who wanted to laugh and smell the outdoors. She did not talk about where she had been. Facing forward, Liz proved to be a good worker. She'd forgotten how much she enjoyed working with her hands.

"Hard to believe that girl wasted herself behind a desk. She's not too bad with a spade,"

Arch observed one evening. "Doesn't mind getting down in the dirt either."

Ruby nodded. "She's in a difficult time right now, Arch," she commented, laying a hand over his for a moment. She passed him the pickled beets she'd brought up from their fruit cellar earlier that evening.

"I think Liz is looking at her troubles and working to overcome them," she added.

Arch, lifting another fork full of roast beef to his mouth, glanced thoughtfully at Ruby and asked, "Did you know this is her birthday? She's thirty-four. Told me so this morning over coffee."

ℰℭ

"No, I do not want to go out and celebrate my birthday, Annie. I'm not in the mood. Really, as far as I'm concerned May fifth is just another day. The kids and I shared cake and ice cream after school and that's enough partying for this old mom," Liz stated firmly.

Annie was not to be dissuaded tonight. Her boyfriend was coming to town from neighboring Pearse and wanted to meet them at the new café and bar downtown. Annie was going and Liz was coming with her.

After she extracted a promise for no fuss, Liz showered and pulled on her favorite pair of jeans and a lavender tee. She ran a brush through her auburn hair, cut blunt to below her ears, and set out on her first sojourn into Benton's night life.

How bad can it be? Liz asked herself. In a town slightly smaller than my high school, how much trouble can I find?

Roger Wallron hadn't arrived yet when they walked into Lots and More, known locally as simply Lots. The place was filling quickly. A large portion of the crowd was couples out on the town and young singles.

The women took a back booth and told the waitress they would wait to order. Glancing around at the customers, Liz noticed a slim, well-built man nearly six foot tall and dressed in dusty cowboy boots, jeans, and a flannel shirt enter Lots and walk up to the bar.

His arms and face were tanned from the outdoors and he was holding a worn cowboy hat in one hand. Light brown hair, streaked blonde from the sun, crept over his shirt collar. Smiling, he listened to a young woman as she walked over to him.

Liz turned her attention back to Annie. Together they watched the bar's patrons and chatted as they waited for Roger. A few minutes later he walked in.

Sliding into the booth next to Annie, he gave her a swift, hard kiss on the lips. Introductions were put on hold when the waitress approached them and took their orders for salads and mega shrimp meals.

Lots was fast becoming famous in the region for its appealing menu, the dance floor, and a well-run bar. It was doing a brisk business this evening with the top twenty country and mainstream pulsating in the background.

Liz sized up the opposition, then soundly chastised herself for thinking in those angry tones. Not everyone was like the people she'd left behind, she thought to herself. The sooner she opened her mind and softened her heart to that fact, the better off she would be. The orders were completed and the waitress departed as swiftly as she'd arrived.

Roger nodded to Liz and with an unadorned hello welcomed her to Nebraska. After visiting for a few minutes, he tried to catch the attention of their waitress. Liz noticed the curly edges of his trimmed, brown hair and decided that, despite his athletic build, he looked like a cuddly bear.

"Would you two like a beer?" he asked, making a move to get up from the booth.

"I'll get it" Liz offered, and to Annie, "How about you?"

"I'll have whatever you're having," Annie answered, pleased at having two of her favorite people there that evening.

Not so bad, Liz thought. Just a night at the new bar in town with your best friend and her guy. What's so tough about that? She was waiting to place her order with the bartender when she noticed someone standing next to her, sipping a beer.

"Evening, ma'am." She turned and saw the dusty cowboy she'd noticed earlier.

"Hi," she said softly.

"Do you come here often?" he asked.

She eyed him for a moment and replied, "No," and then the bartender was in front of her, taking her order.

Watching her as she juggled three beer mugs and a billfold he spoke again, "Want a little help there, ma'am?"

"No thank you."

He paused a moment, then amused, "Need a little help there?"

She looked up and seeing his grin, frowned. "I thought I already said 'no thanks.'"

"I was just pointing out the difference between want and need. No offense." He nodded to her as she turned her back on him and returned to her table.

"Who's that?" Annie asked, curious about whom her friend knew from the local crowd.

"I have no idea," she murmured, looking back toward the bar. She noticed him look over, smile suddenly, and walk toward them. "But it appears as though that's one cowboy who's not giving up."

Roger chuckled as the man slid onto the bench next to Liz. "Hassling my guest?"

"Just making conversation, Rog," he answered, settling his hat on his knee and reaching over to shake Liz's hand, then Annie's. Roger introduced Jay Robbins to the women.

"Jay just moved back to Benton a few months ago," Roger explained. "We've known each other since our high school football days on opposite sides of the line. Have I ever told you how much I enjoyed bashing you back then?" he asked Jay, a big grin lighting up his face.

"I don't remember it that way," Jay shot back. He looked closely at Annie. "We ran into each other years ago when I was home visiting." He reminded her of the summer she'd been waiting tables at a local restaurant and had quit in the middle of his family's order. He asked about her grandparents and the Dirt Store.

Liz's gaze was drawn out the window, past the parking lot, to waves of pasture grass blowing in the distance. Folding over one another, the grasses were playing leap frog, chickening out yet again and again.

The waves gave up their game and started a new one. And then another. The sun's reflection on the pasture drew distinct hues of green from each plant, making the whole scene shimmery, unreal.

Liz's attention jolted back to the booth as Jay spoke again. "I was saying I'm sorry if I was being rude over there." His smirk seemed intact.

She responded with a cool smile. "Not at all. I'm just new to the area and not accustomed to speaking to strangers in a bar. That would be a very dangerous move where I come from."

"Where would that be?"

"Minneapolis," she said shortly.

He tried again. "How do you like it here?"

"Fine."

Jay reached for his brim.

"Stay and eat with us?" Roger offered.

"Thanks anyway, but I'll leave you three to your visit." Jay then stood, tipping his hat to Liz, she ignoring his humored glance. He left the bar a while later.

Liz concentrated on their three-way conversation. She could see how Annie, after returning to her roots to take a teaching job, had found Roger. He had a quality about him like that of a trusted old friend. And he was funny, entertaining them thoroughly with a story of his co-workers' shock several months earlier when he'd announced he was moving out of Boston and into this little piece of the world.

He could still work via telecommunications technology. Since his contributions had been increasingly important to the computer engineering firm over the past half dozen years, his company had bent over backwards to accommodate his move.

Liz and Annie chuckled as Roger mimicked company coffee machine conversations about why and how in the world. But he'd done it. He moved back to his hometown where his parents and sister's family still lived.

Annie met Roger when he volunteered to do some computer consulting at the high school where she taught English and speech. She was immediately attracted to the handsome, somewhat serious man who loved sports and was patient with the computer illiterate.

"The part I love is where your co-workers claim everything is so slow paced here. Where, I ask, is the slow lane so I can get in it?" Annie challenged with a snort. "Since the day I moved back to Benton, I've been teaching and coaching the speech team. I got roped into a fund raiser for the park renovation. I go to Kearney once a week for supplies for Gran and Gramp's store and I'll be coaching a girls softball team this summer. Practices on Sunday afternoons and two games a week. Show me slow!" she pleaded.

"I remember when I told people I was moving here," Liz offered quietly.

Roger looked at her thoughtfully. "Thought you were nuts, right?"

"My folks said the same thing," Annie said. "And they grew up here!" Their salads arrived followed shortly by their shrimp platters.

As they ate, Liz decided her problems were in her mind. Despite trying hard to immerse herself into a new place and new work, she was finding it harder to recreate herself than she'd anticipated when she'd sat up late at night in Minneapolis, dreaming of a new start.

Most days she doubted she was up to the challenge. She loved the Morrisons and the Dirt Store. There she was meeting people who were genuine. It was when the sun set and the worry bugs crawled out of the seamless corners, that she was in trouble. The kids, though, and their fights and new friendships were helping to occupy her mind.

And Annie and Roger were fun to watch. Right now they were grinning at one another, but they also reminded her of Minneapolis. She entered their conversation, anxious to cut off her own thoughts.

ഇൻൻ

School let out a couple weeks later. Swim lessons, Ben's peewee baseball games, lawn and garden work at Annie's, the Dirt Store; Liz was exhausted every night and grateful for it.

Often now she lay in bed reading late into the night, forcing new ideas, exotic settings into her mind. She concentrated on the characters, the plot, what she would do differently if she was the author, anything other than herself.

But her dreams weren't always gentle ones. Too often her old life came crashing through the whispery moonlight and into her upstairs bedroom windows. Even on the nights when she slept well, she'd drag through her day, tired from the stress of worry about her future.

Tess had gone with her to the Dirt Store during the first few weeks they'd lived in Benton. Now that Annie was out of school for the summer, Tess usually followed her around. Liz was a little less tied down and grateful to her friend for stepping in to help out.

Thursday night toward the beginning of June she, Annie, and the girls were in the stands watching Ben's team finish their game with nearby Trenton. It was that sultry, tight kind of hot evening when everyone wished it would just get it over with and thunder and lightning and kick up a big storm, sending everyone scurrying to their cars.

Clouds were building in the west and the sun pounded down on them as they climbed to seats in the top row of the bleachers to cheer for Ben and his teammates. In a little while, when the sun dropped a little more, the evening's breezes could just as easily have them wishing they had jackets in their cars.

Liz noticed Roger and his friend from the bar as they drove up and jogged out onto the adjoining field. They were warming up with several members of the town's fast pitch softball team. Between batters she glanced over and saw them clowning around, enjoying the workout with their teammates.

"What you looking at, girl? Got your eye on my man?" Annie lowered her voice. "Or maybe his buddy?"

She chuckled softly as Liz jerked her attention back to Ben's game and muttered to the infield "Not I, said the chicken. I'm here to watch Benjo play ball. Period."

A week later Liz was picking up her daughters from swim lessons and dropping Ben off for his class when she saw Jay again, this time with an attractive brunette. They drove by in a pickup, pulling a trailer with two horses.

He waved as they met but she ignored the gesture, driving on to drop the girls at Annie's and then going back to work. Liz's annulment papers from the morning's mail were still sitting on her work desk at The Dirt Store, making her divorce last year all the more real. Social pleasantries this morning were a secondary concern.

And then she didn't notice Jay for several weeks. Maybe he was around and she was just too busy or too tired to know it. Annie warned her to slow down a little, to take it easy. "You're getting thin, Liz. You're worn out. Why don't you take a day off?" After similar comments from the Morrisons, she did.

She got up late and ate a cereal breakfast with her kids as they sprawled across the living room floor. They watched a cartoon tape for a while and messed around in the backyard for the rest of the morning.

At noon, she packed a picnic and they walked the few blocks to the park in their swimsuits and shorts, barefoot and in high spirits. The day would constitute the family vacation this year, she suddenly realized, a tear forming in her eye. She kicked a stone with her toe, thinking how it was still an improvement over the family trips to those lovely resorts of her past life.

Suddenly she saw Jay standing in front of her, talking to the brunette from the pickup. She wiped at the dampness on her cheek and said hello. He nodded, his eyes following her as he continued visiting with his companion.

Liz kept walking. She caught up with her children at a picnic table shaded by a towering cottonwood. Laying out the food and passing paper plates around, she was too busy to notice the woman and three children leave the park.

But when she heard a diesel engine start, she turned in time to see Jay drive around the corner of the park and stop at the intersection. He leaned out of his window to talk with a middle-aged man who had been driving in the opposite direction. Soon Jay's pickup truck drove off. The look on the face of the second man was hard to see but she got the impression he was angry.

Seventeen months fresh from a divorce made her feel grateful for a nice, quiet swim with her kids. Trust your instincts, Liz told herself. He's trouble. And you don't need any.

ℰℛ

Ben walked through the front door and studied the scene, a tiny trail left with each step. The house at the edge of Benton was undergoing some serious renovation, with old and new lumber piled outside and power tool noises coming from inside. He had decided to take a look before heading home to what would likely be an indoor squall.

He wasn't just dirty. Dirt alone couldn't possibly be blamed for the damage done to his new jeans and tennis shoes. This was a nine-year-old's special concoction of dirt, sand, and grass, mixed maybe with an old fire's cinder remnants.

"Hand me that saw to your east, would you?" A man was standing at the top of the winding staircase. He didn't seem to notice the clumps of dirt around the boy's feet.

Ben picked up the saw and brought it up the steps, hoping to sneak a peek at the second story. "Mind if I take a look around, now that I'm up here?"

"Now that you're up here, go ahead."

The boy sucked in his breath. Standing in the center of the spacious room, he kept looking, turning slowly in a complete circle. Twisting his stained ball cap in his grimy hands, Ben's dark hair shot out in several directions. A recent scrape, the blood now dried, was evident on his cheekbone.

"Wow, this is great! Doin' this by yourself?" Ben asked. He forgot about the storm expected at home surely precipitated by his filthy arrival, and more closely examined the room's views: the hills to the west, the town of Benton, the new spring lawn grass growing in unruly tufts.

A herd of red cows and their young calves, all with white faces, grazed in a nearby pasture. A calf bucked, kicking both hind legs up and to the side, then skittered away.

"I'm on my own with this project. Long way to go, huh?" The man nodded at the room, assuming the agreement of Ben.

Ben agreed. "Yeah. Use some help? I'm pretty good with tools. I help Mom out all the time."

The man leaned back against a wall, sized the boy up, and thought a few moments. Ben, looking the man straight in the eye, bore the scrutiny well.

"All right, you're in. Show up when you want, help me with what you can, take off when you're bored. How's that sound for a job description?" he asked, smiling to himself.

"Sounds good to me," Ben said. Taking the steps two at a time, he ran down the staircase and out the front door.

The scene he had imagined was far worse than it actually played when he arrived home. His dad would have been furious with him, all right. He always seemed to look for things to find wrong with Ben.

Liz looked him over from head to toe, shook her head wearily, and ordered him straight back to the sun porch to shed his clothes and to shower off his grime.

Liz returned to Annie and their conversation. "So you and Roger are getting pretty close?"

"We are," Annie nodded, "and I'm probably as surprised as he is at that. Talk about opposites. I'm so, you know, loud, spur-of-the-moment. He's a techie, for God's sake."

She laughed delightedly. "But he is so much fun and such a good guy. And a very romantic man, I might add" pursing her lips into a pleased expression.

Seeing the look on her friend's face, Annie reached out to shake Liz's shoulder. "Come on, Lizzy, romance isn't dead." Quietly she added, "It's just on hold for you right now."

"On hold? I don't think so, Annie. I'm living out my life raising my kids, working, and giving very wide berth to male types in general. Oh, except maybe Arch. Your Grandpa is wonderful."

Joyfully feeling the hot water washing away his worries, Ben took another step toward healing. His Mom wasn't the only person who was glad they'd come to this little town in the middle of nowhere. Everything was different here. It was like the good stuff in people came out more and the bad stuff was dealt with and then forgotten.

Back in Minneapolis Ben would have caught it big- time if he'd come home looking like he did tonight, from both Mom and Dad. His dad was never satisfied with anything he did, and it kind of spilled over to his mom's treatment of him, too. On the other hand, where would he have been allowed to go to have found that much dirt in the first place?

During supper Ben announced he'd met a man who was fixing up an old house. Liz looked up slowly from her plate.

He was just some poor guy, Ben said, who had a house with a really cool upstairs. It sure looked like he could use a hand, and the man had even offered him a job.

"You went in? To a stranger's house? Benjamin John, you know better than that!" Liz said angrily, her eyes snapping.

He sat still.

"Who is he?" Liz asked.

"I don't know."

She sighed. "Ben, I can't have you running around with people we don't know."

"Mom, I'm not running around. I'd just be helping him fix up a run-down old house."

Liz let out her breath. "Honey, that's what I mean."

"Oh, Mom, this ain't Minneapolis!"

"Isn't."

"See, you agree. So can I? Please?"

He's always been good at this, Liz reminded herself, determined not to get drawn into debating with a nine-year-old child with a penchant for adventure.

Communications may have been her field but Ben had always had this gift for chipping away at her objections. "I suppose it wouldn't hurt, but..." Ben froze in the middle of a silent cheer..."Oh honey, I don't know."

She thought a moment. "First, I'll need to know who it is. Then, I need to know when you're going there and when you get home, whether I'm here or at the Dirt Store. If you can work all that out," she eyed him seriously, "I suppose it would be okay."

Later that evening, after Annie left for a movie with Roger, Liz was standing at the kitchen sink. She idly scrubbed the broiler pan, her thoughts drifting past the backyard and the alley beyond.

How simple it is for Ben. A man needs help and her young son volunteers. And Jane. She walks across the street to play with two sisters every day after lunch. Tess follows Annie around as she readies her classroom for the new year.

As for me, she thought, I wait on mostly pleasant people every single day. I love the simplistic beauty of feeling comfortable about what I'm doing, about what my kids are doing.

Still, I can't seem to trust that everything's going to be okay. I keep looking for the expiration date, the disclaimer.

Maybe that's a sign of shallow living for too long. I've evidently learned to trust no one except those who've proven beyond a shadow of a doubt that I can trust them. And that's a pretty short list; those I've known since my childhood, and since their childhood.

It's not that I didn't have good people in my life before. But there was this fragile edge around me, like little pieces of brittle clothing. I sometimes felt I had to walk just so or I'd end up naked. As it turned out, that's what happened anyway. I was naked after all and no one told me.

At the sound of the doorbell Tess and Jane ran to the sun porch, both tripping over Ben's pile of clothing and landing hard against the unlatched screen door. Out of the porch they tumbled and would have crashed on the sidewalk if not for a pair of tanned arms.

"Who is it?" Liz called out from the kitchen, reaching for a hand towel.

Jane called back. "I don't know, Mom, but he's pretty strong." Reflexes kicking in, Liz charged the door.

Jay took a step backward, letting the girls down on stable ground and giving their mom space. It seemed to help.

She said hello as the girls stood watching. When she didn't invite him in, he invited her out to Annie's lawn chairs.

Liz hesitated. Then as she finished drying her hands with the dish towel, "Would you like something to drink? A glass of water, or some soda?"

"No thanks. I just wanted to talk to you for a minute about a business proposition I have in mind. Is this a good time?"

"A what?" Liz asked. "Has Annie been telling you what I do?" They sat down.

"A business proposition," Jay repeated. "I think it was your son who stumbled in on my remodeling mess today and felt sorry for me. He offered to help me out. I could use a second set of hands if you don't mind. I thought I'd stop by and see if that would be all right."

So it was Jay. "You know, he mentioned something about a building project at dinner."

"What did you tell him?" Jay asked, curious if her attitude toward him had improved since the night at Lots.

"I told him I'd think about it." She shifted in her chair, uncomfortable in the conversation. "Where is this house?"

"If you have a few minutes, I'll show you." He noticed a slight stiffening in her shoulders even as she nodded.

She told Tess and Jane to stay by the house, and then looked back at Jay as he waited. "How far is it?"

ℰⁿℭ

"He surprised me," Liz told Annie the next morning. "I guess after meeting him in the bar and seeing him around town I expected something else."

"Like what?" The women were hiking, spending the last weekend of summer break out of doors.

"Oh, I don't know. He seemed so cocky in the bar, a lady's man. Kind of like he hadn't a care or responsibility in the world. Last night he was just very quiet, and polite."

"Polite. That's it? Polite?"

"Annie, we walked three blocks, looked at the house a minute or two, and then I went home. Polite is all I noticed."

"Hmm, I noticed more in the bar," Annie said, as she examined one of her polished fingernails. "Like how the women stopped to talk with him and how the men enjoyed being with him, too."

Liz gave her friend a deadly look. "Did I fail to mention my husband left me because I'm not lovable? Kind of hard to forget that little tidbit stuck in your portfolio."

"Liz, that's ridiculous and you know it. Ever since we met you've been the one person I could always count on to know where she stood, what was what. Sometimes I think you unnerve, even threaten people because you are so confident, so capable. Your ex is simply trying to bury you to pump himself up. It's a damn shame you married him. But I know we've already discussed that topic and we don't need to cover old ground, including the part where I told you so."

Annie shook her head and pointed at Liz before she could open her mouth. "Don't bother," and then turning around to survey the canyon below them, "What do you say we hike this next canyon and then head for home?" Annie strode off.

"Wait," Liz said, hurrying to catch up. Annie looked back.

"All I'm saying is he acted decent last night and I believe I can trust Ben around him. That's all I'm saying."

"Oh," Annie said coolly.

"What now?" Liz asked, exasperated.

"Just wondering if it would kill you to simply say you liked the guy. Forget it," Annie threw up her hands and shook her head a second time. "I'm not going to argue with you, Lizzie. You've got to live your life your way. Come on, let's finish this canyon."

ᏘᏟ

"I've never met a woman who carried herself so quietly, like she didn't want anyone knocking on the door and coming in," Jay told Roger. They were moving some equipment around in the office and den additions Jay had built for Roger's home, and enjoying fresh rolls with their Saturday morning project.

"She didn't really want to go with me and I don't think it was because she's not that wild about me either," Jay said with a grin, "Although that's true enough. She just kind of pulled herself together and we walked over. What do you know about her?"

Roger considered the question. "All I know is what Annie said several weeks ago when she was excited about her friend moving to Benton." He shoved his desk closer to the large window. "That she wanted to come here to breathe fresh air and lots of it."

"She started to say something last night and dropped it, something about the work she did before." Jay was digging for information and this came as a surprise to both of them. Finished with their work, they moved outside onto the screened porch where the shade trees helped to screen them from the warming day. The neighborhood kids were playing soccer with reckless abandon, their summer vacation ebbing madly away.

"I think she was in public relations in Minneapolis," Roger said. He frowned at Jay. "Since when don't you just ask a woman when you want to know something? What happened last night, anyway?"

"It's funny," Jay mused, scratching the back of his neck as he looked around the neighborhood. "I've dated several women. Nothing serious ever developed under the best of circumstances. I move back here where everybody knows everybody and I meet an attractive, spirited woman. She wasn't the only one nervous last night."

He glanced at Roger. "What happened?" He shrugged. "Nothing. We walked over to the house and I turned on the lights. I watched her look around downstairs. She was there a couple of minutes and said it would be fine with her for Ben to help me out."

Jay finished his roll and reached for his coffee. "Then she said she'd better be heading home to check on her kids and she took off. I wanted her to stay and talk. But I could tell that I needed to just let her walk out."

He glanced at Roger's face, gauging his reaction to his next comment. "Conventional knowledge would say that the big city, lots of choice, educated, sophisticated, good matches. But I never found it that way. It was more to sift through. More pretense, more games."

"I know what you mean," Roger nodded. "I'm wondering what Annie's going to say when I ask her to marry me."

Jay jerked his head to the side, his eyes sharp on Roger.

Roger went on. "She likes her independence but then I think, hell, why did any of us move back here? It wasn't for better jobs or better money. There's no professional sports or major entertainment in Pearse. It takes me two hours just to get to the airport to travel to consultations. But this is where I intend to stay. I know Annie does. I'll bet you do, too."

Roger sipped from his coffee, smiling at the soccer game next door which was slowly but surely deteriorating into a scramble of body parts. The air was punctuated with grunts and shouts from the battle.

"I can just hear everyone back in Boston," he said. "About giving in, finding whoever I can, and just settling down because I'm getting older and want someone. And they're right. Except the part about giving in and finding just anyone. If I'd met Annie in the city I'd have wanted her there, too."

The kids were now kicking one another nearly as often as the soccer ball. The youngest of the group, a wiry little redhead, with a Cornhusker headband and in shorts a couple sizes too large, was in the thick of it and having the time of his life.

"I'll tell you something," Roger said, eying Jay. "Liz's kids were with Annie the other day and ended up eating lunch with us. They helped set the table without being asked, talked about what they were doing this summer. The boy, Ben, is a great kid."

"He's got character, all right," Jay agreed. "He looked me square in the eye yesterday when he asked if he could help."

"That's him," Roger nodded. "And the girls are the same. Smart, quick to catch on, and they're definitely female in a good kind of way. Annie thinks they're great. Says she likes her friend even more for them. Unsolicited as it may be, I've got a little advice for you."

Roger reached for the box of rolls with one hand and opened the screened porch door with the other. "Something stung her and the bee doesn't look to have died just yet. You may have to wait until it's dead or even help kill it. I guess that's why she's here, to beat the bee to death."

Jay caught the screen door before it could bang shut. "Some advice," he said dryly. "Who said I was interested in seeing her?"

From inside: "I wasn't the one digging."

৪০৫৪

Tess's first day of school came and went. Several firsts were accomplished as Benton's class of twenty-one kindergartners hurtled into the expansive world of formal education with Mrs. Bryson.

Ben and Jane had looked forward to the start of school. They already knew their class-mates from last spring and from a golden summer spent at the pool, tearing around the neighborhood, and at Ben's baseball games.

Tess had gotten to know some classmates during the summer, as well.

Liz was amazed at how smoothly the school year began and how content her family was, despite homework and the loss of summer's license. They fell into the routine of school, work, and homework. The Dirt Store continued to be a place of rejuvenation for Liz.

Benton, small and surrounded by postcard-like settings, was having an effect on her. She slept a little better, worried a little less, and had taken to thinking in terms of days instead of months or years.

Some of this Liz attributed to Arch and Ruby. Their quiet example gave her quite a little food for thought. She had also adopted a strict rule of surrounding herself with only positive people. It seemed to be working.

Some mornings after the kids left for their short walk to school, she'd bike a few miles out of town. Each time she'd try a new road, examining the contours of the hills and canyons, committing to memory the different shades of grasses and wildflowers, noting new bird songs.

Liz was like the kid let loose for the first time on a beach or near a mountain creek, fascinated by the lush colors, sounds, scents. Then she'd haul herself back to town to work, refreshed.

The demons from her life in Minneapolis were deliberately being purged, one at a time. Mornings she woke to relative silence; no more fire alarms, garbage trucks, traffic helicopters, or neighbors leaving home in the dark only to return in the dark.

Today she was pedaling as fast as she could. Having forgotten her watch, she was concerned she'd be late for work a second day in a row. The Morrisons didn't pay attention to the clock, but her own desire to pull her weight and earn her paycheck were enough to make her bear down and pump hard.

When the front tire went down she knew she should have steered clear of the weeds pulled to the middle of the gravel road by the grader. The puncture vine surely had gotten her, also the second day in a row.

Liz was pushing her bike toward Benton when an old pickup truck pulled alongside her and Jay leaned out the window. "You know, if you get on it and pedal it you'll get where you're going a whole lot faster." He laughed at her expression. "What? Doesn't anyone tease you?"

He turned off the ignition and stepped out, reaching for her bike when she quietly answered. "Actually, no," she said, and then looked more closely at the pickup he was driving. "Do you have a different truck for each day of the week?"

Laying her bike carefully on the truck's flatbed, he opened his door and smiled. "I just drive whatever's handy when I'm out checking pastures. Don't want to run my new one through ditches and over gopher mounds."

He waited, hands on hips and in a calm, amused voice spoke. "Liz, if you want me to give your bike a ride into town and leave you to walk, fine by me. But you have to admit, it's going to look pretty stupid."

She silently studied his expression, then stepped onto the running board and slid over to the passenger side. Jay got back in and turned the key. After a couple attempts the ignition fired.

"Thank you," she said quietly. "I appreciate your taking the time to do this. I didn't want to be late for work again." He sat idling the truck, waiting for the gas to work it's way smoothly through the line.

"Again? You make a habit of it?" She laughed, despite herself and he grinned back. Pushing his hat back from his forehead, he apologized. "But something about you makes me want to pick at you. Maybe it's how you look so calm, in charge all the time. Just bugs a country boy like myself."

"Something tells me you're not what you seem," she returned, looking at him as if for the first time. His innocent eyes made her laugh again.

"Where to?" he asked as he revved the motor.

"Home, please."

Jay had shifted into low when a pickup slowed its approach and stopped opposite his door. The window slid down and the man from the park leaned out.

"Morning, Jay."

"Gordie."

"Didn't get a chance to visit last night after the meeting," Gordie commented. He rubbed his glistening forehead against his shirt sleeve, waiting for Jay to speak.

"Didn't figure it would do any good," Jay said, a firm set to his jaw.

"Now, you're not going to be difficult over this little thing, are you?"

"Only if you are, Gordie. It's your call."

Gordie stared hard at Jay, then drove off in a cloud of dust, kicking gravel off the roadbed and back onto the pickup.

Jay shifted the truck into low gear once again but left his foot on the clutch. Eyes on the road, both hands firm on the wheel, he asked Liz, "Aren't you going to ask what that was about?"

"I usually keep my nose out of other people's business," she answered, studying his profile. He nodded his head slowly, and after glancing in his rear view mirror, drove into town.

When they reached Annie's rental house, Jay deposited his passenger, honking as he drove off. No, you're not what you seem, Mr. Robbins, Liz told herself. Just what you are is unclear.

A few days later Liz was searching for her eldest. "Did you see Ben on your way home?" Liz asked as Annie walked in from a long day of warm classrooms and speech tryouts.

Annie shook her head. "Why?"

Liz crossed her arms. "I don't know where he is. The girls said he came home after school and tore into the fridge, jumped into his old clothes, and was back out the door in under two minutes. He left them to carry his backpack and instrument in off the lawn."

Ten days into the new school year, Liz was already having to go looking for Ben and drag him home to supper. At least in Minneapolis she had always known where Ben was. Where could he have gone without her?

I suppose I'm not really worried about him so much as I'm annoyed I've got to hunt him down for supper and face his boss at the same time, Liz told herself. I just want Benton, the kids, and Ben's new used trombone. If I'm honest with myself, though, that's not the real issue here.

He's nice looking, he's single, and he's three blocks away. He thoughtfully fixed my tire and returned my bike to the front lawn before I got back from work. Ben thinks he's great. The girls think he's like a country western star without the glitter and guitar.

What do I think? It doesn't matter. I'm just getting so I can sleep well at night after months of tossing and turning. I'm not getting into that mess again. The rest of my life may not be the romantic picture I imagined as a little girl but it won't be the painful corner of hell it turned into either. And for that, I'll gladly pay the price of a kind of neutral existence.

Liz studied her image in the hall mirror. Remember, you were divorced by your husband because he didn't think he loved you. Don't trust anyone with anything except maybe the grocery store scanners. And even those you better watch. Come on, get it over with. Go get your boy and get home.

Ben spied his mother from an upper window and begged Jay to stand up for him if things got a little rough. Jay chuckled, wondering how he'd passed the time before running into this neat little guy.

"Mind if I come in?" Liz called through the open front door.

"We're upstairs." Jay's head appeared at the top of the winding staircase. "Watch your step. Nails are all over."

"Wow." Liz cast her eyes around the sun-flooded room, admiring the new windows, flooring, and woodwork. "I didn't see much my first visit. This is really nice." He accepted her compliment, at ease as he watched her look around the room.

"Ben," she said, turning her full attention on her son, "the deal was you tell me where you are going before you go. Now it's time to get home and help with supper. The girls weren't too thrilled about the pack mule job you gave them."

"Um, Mom, Jay wanted me to come as soon as I could, right Jay?"

With hopeful eyes, Ben held his breath, waiting for help out of unwanted chores and for the chance to be just guys.

"He is good help and I appreciate your lending him to me, Liz. But," turning to the boy, "your main job is school and home. When it's okay with your mom, it's fine with me. But her jobs come first. Better head home, pal."

Ben, kicking at a pile of sawdust with his toe, reluctantly headed toward the winding stairs. He walked past his mom and looked back at his friend with a half abandoned, half still-pleased look. "See ya, Jay. Beat ya home, Mom!" Then he was down the steps and gone.

Liz started for the staircase, then paused. "Thank you. He's been testing my authority lately." She slid her hands deep into her jeans pockets, glancing about the room once more. "This really is quite good work," she said, filling the void. "Who's the designer?" Jay crossed his arms, smiling broadly. "You? You do this?"

She walked to a window and surveyed the hills in the distance, the sidewalk below. She stammered as she turned back to face him. "I thought you, I didn't know you, ...I..." and seeing his enjoyment at her confusion, "...ah, damn."

He laughed outright as she shot him a mortified look. "I am so sorry," she said softly. "I thought you were a cowboy working on some ranch like a lot of the men I've met since I moved here. Not that there's a thing wrong with that," she hastily added as he raised a brow. "Really, I'm not a career chauvinist. But I had no idea you did this type of work. What's with the trucks and trailers?"

He told her he'd grown up on a ranch nearby and was helping out in between jobs. On a deeper level, she listened to how he talked to her.

"So you've made the acquaintance of Benton's finest have you?" he asked. She frowned, not understanding. "The singles crowd."

"Oh that. Well, I seem to bump into them."

"I'll bet you do," Jay murmured. He changed the subject. "If you're interested, sometime I could show you my plans for this old place."

"That would be nice," she said politely. Liz glanced sideways as she walked past where he was leaning against the bannister. "Can I ask you something?" She took a few steps down.

"Go ahead." He turned and rested his hands on the top railing, looking down at her.

"Did you really ask Ben to hike it over after school?"

Jay matched her look and repeated, "He really is good help."

ഇൻൻ

"King, king, come on. Nowhere to go. Okay, three of spades? Nope. Ten of hearts. On the Jack. Nine over on the ten. Good."

Annie walked in carrying a stack of books and papers to grade. "I'm surprised you beat me home. Couldn't Gran and Grandad find enough for you to do today?"

Liz ignored this. She was in a magnanimous mood this evening. "They decided to quit early. We're all worn out."

"Do I ever remember that. Fall planting season comes close to spring for marathon hours," Annie said, dropping her load on a side table and sliding onto the floor next to Liz's chair. Then she laughed when she saw the solitaire game on the screen. "Are you at that again?"

"I know you think this is ridiculous, but I think it is interesting. I can play the same game over and over and each time, with a slightly different play, it turns out so unlike the one before." She pushed the keyboard back and looked at her friend.

Amused, Annie shook her head. "You know, I think it's time for you to do something besides work the counter at the store. You're getting a little stale up there," she said, pointing to Liz's head.

"I did. Today. Beth Matthews ordered several bulbs and wanted us to put them in. She said her knees were getting worse and it was worth it to her to pay us and still be able to enjoy the flowers next spring. Your grandad tilled and I planted about three hundred tulips and daffodils this afternoon. Plenty of time to think. Then Ben came tearing by asking if he could borrow some money. He's already spent the money Jay paid him for working."

Liz turned off her computer. "Seems he overheard Roger and Jay talking about Jay's birthday coming up and Ben wants to get him something."

Shifting her chair to the side, Liz turned to face Annie. She seemed to decide something. "I need to get my own place," she began. "My eyes are open to the fact that we're happy enough in Benton to settle in some more. Besides, you need your space back." Liz ignored her friend's protest. "I'm serious. Who else would have taken the four of us in with only a couple weeks notice and let us live here for the past five months? You've been wonderful."

A quick intake of breath and she continued. "Now I want to give you back your privacy. It's time for me to settle into my own place."

Annie gave this some thought, then winked. "Well. It's about time. Got any leads? Benton is undergoing a rental boom. What with me and you, housing is really getting crunched."

"I was thinking about that old house with the red door a mile outside of town. I saw it when I was biking a few days ago. I hadn't gone down that way before."

Liz tugged a pillow off the sofa and dropped to the floor. She told Annie that the house's drapes were drawn so Liz couldn't see in. "But I think we could move in and fix it up slowly, a little at a time. Hopefully the owners won't want too much rent. What do you think?"

Later that evening, with a full moon rising, Ben and Jane away at friends homes for overnights, and Annie in Kearney with some teacher friends for dinner and a movie, Tess and Liz were popping corn and enjoying one another's company.

Tess had just asked a question when Liz, mid-sentence, was interrupted by the doorbell and then a knock at the door. Stepping out onto the screened porch, she met Jay's gaze.

"Jay. Hello."

"Mind if I come in?" he asked. Tess came to the door, lifted the latch, and taking his hand guided him to the leather sofa.

"We're having popcorn and looking for a good show on TV, but Mom says that most of it is just junk. She said she wants to watch a spider eat a fly instead. Have you ever seen that? Is it really cool?"

Tess sat down, tugging on his hand for him to sit next to her. Liz felt a trickle of panic run through her veins at the thought of Jay staying and her control of the situation dwindling.

"Liz, you are one lucky woman. Ben is such a great kid. And this one, Tess is it? How old are you?" Tess raised her hand. "Five? I would have guessed ten at least, maybe eleven."

The girl giggled, then she slid off the sofa and ran to her room, no doubt searching out some wonderful show and tell item.

Please God, let it be presentable. And while you're at it, Liz thought, would you get this man out of my home? "What are you doing here?" she asked, aware of how that sounded.

He gave her an exaggerated look. "Roger has something cooked up for my birthday. Based on what I organized for him last year, this is going to be a night to remember. And I'd just as soon not. How about you hide me out and let Rog explain to his cohorts about a party minus the guest?"

She didn't miss a beat. "You know, Jay, if I didn't know any better and if I hadn't been out of the loop for several years now, I'd say that was the most lame excuse for a reason to come over here and see me tonight that I've heard in ages." She expected he would now leave. He did not.

"You know, Liz, I can see how it might look that way, but..."

"You know what you sound like?" she interrupted, amused. "Like those awful telemarketers who call at all times of the day and night from anonymous phone numbers and as soon as you catch on to what they're after and say 'no thanks', they say how they sure can understand how you could feel that way, but…"

There was another pause and then they both laughed at the absurdity of their conversation.

Jay glanced around the room, seeing school books, shoes, and a basketball. It was obvious a family lived here. "I need to tell you something, Liz. I hope you won't mind if I just say what's on my mind. That's the only way I know how to talk."

"Really? I hadn't noticed," she murmured.

But he was serious now. "Ever since I met you last spring, I've felt like I'm back in high school and you're the girl I want to ask to the dance. But I can't quite figure out how to do it. I get the distinct feeling that you're not going to say yes."

"I think that's my fault" she answered, embarrassed now that the talk had taken this turn. She bit her lip. "I am uncomfortable in my own skin these days and I think I make other people nervous about what to say or do because even I don't know what to say or do. I am extremely edgy right now, to put it mildly." She dropped her voice. "Frankly, it's a lot easier to just stay away from people."

"Afraid to make a mistake?" His observant question was unsettling to her.

She looked at him sharply, sizing him up anew. "Not so much that," she answered slowly, "I just don't have the energy to survive many more." He waited, thinking he had not often heard so much honesty in so few words.

"Tell you what," she relaxed slightly, "stay and visit this evening and we'll cooperate in the cover-up. Who knows, maybe I'm not the girl you want to take to the dance after all," she said. I don't dance anymore, she told herself. Liz gestured to the sofa as she sat opposite him.

Tess reappeared. In tow were old slippers which, she whispered to Jay, were her mom's cast offs. Jay examined them with great interest and chuckled when Liz suggested Tess had probably shared enough and would she please take them back to her room now.

Then one of Tess' favorite Disney movies came on and she settled down on the floor with her bowl of popcorn. The adults were left to their words.

"I'm interested in knowing how you came to Benton, about what you did back in Minneapolis," he ventured. "Mind if I ask?"

"Actually, it's kind of strange to be asked about my past. I used to live it, not remember it." She walked out to Annie's kitchen and brought Jay a bowl of popcorn. Then Liz sat and quietly gave shape to her thoughts.

She stared at the TV and began talking. "Mike and I got married when I was twenty-four and he was almost thirty. We met when I was doing a PR consultation for his company. That's what I do," she glanced over at Jay, "communications and public relations. He was a young exec zooming up the corporate ladder and I just knew we were in love. I guess I was in love as much as you can be with someone who doesn't really love you back."

He studied her face but her emotions remained hidden. "Ben was born the end of our second year together. I took some time off from work but basically we both drove hard and I kept things together at home. The pressure should have eased off as the babies grew older and I found good at-home care for them. But it didn't work out that way."

Her brows creased slightly as she continued. "I finally realized that Mike loved money and working and the kill more than he loved me. Or the kids. He kind of floated by us, in and out of our lives, but he didn't ever really take part in it. More like a visitor than a committed adult, I guess.

"Don't get me wrong. I'm no saint." She laughed sharply at this. "My ego loved my job, and the perks that come with the money and title." She paused, looked out the window into the darkness, and then reluctantly back at Jay.

"But I loved my children. I was so disappointed in a husband who would look at me with something bordering on indifference. He didn't have affairs, Jay. Mike didn't even care enough to do that. He just plain didn't care. Mike didn't know how to be close to someone. He wouldn't give one more minute to me or us than he absolutely had to; it was as if anything that took time he didn't want to give was just too damn low on his list."

Her anger could be seen in her flashing eyes and hands clenched tightly in her lap. She shook her hair back from her face and checked to see that Tess was still involved in her show. Drawing a ragged breath, Liz went on but in a slower, softer voice.

"So I told him that I wanted to quit work and stay home to be there for him and the kids. I wanted to make it work. When Mike said he'd think about it, I got excited. I honestly believed that this discomfort, this ache in our lives that I'd always sensed, would finally go away. Maybe now we'd be better and I'd feel whole. Somehow I'd found the broken piece and could mend it. Boy, wasn't I something?" The music from the commercial was loud, forming a bridge from her last word to her next.

Jay's eyes remained steady on her face. When Tess asked for more popcorn, Liz went out to the kitchen for another bowlful. After the girl became absorbed in the show, Liz studied Jay.

"One day Mike came home and said he wanted out, that he wasn't happy. He wasn't sure he loved me and he wanted to start a new life for himself. Without me. I was shocked. Devastated. I was so angry that he could just throw me, it, all of us away and think that all that would change would be his address."

She lifted tear laced eyes to his, certain she'd told him far more than he cared to know. Angry red marks rode high on her cheekbones. She looked vulnerable and invincible all at once. ✳

"What did you do?" he asked simply.

She shrugged, and grimacing, told him the rest. "I stayed in Minneapolis. I worked up until the divorce was final, accepted the sympathy people sent my way, and continued to live in our townhouse." She shook her head, remembering.

She had tried to keep everything low-key with the kids so that nothing would seem altered; nothing except that their father had walked out on all of them with little thought for the consequences of their breakup.

"And I stayed at work. I figured at least this way we didn't need to go through any other changes in our lives. Mike saw the kids occasionally but neither he nor they minded when he forgot or their plans didn't work out."

"We kept on for about a year and a half that way before I woke up one morning and admitted I was absolutely miserable. I started looking around for some place to go and start over. One day Annie called and mentioned her grandparents' store. Two days later I turned in my notice and was so ridiculously grateful to leave all that behind me it was pathetic."

She looked directly at him and slowly exhaled. "I really like working at the Dirt Store. I really like having real, meaningful relationships, and I'm going to fiercely protect myself from anything that smacks of fake."

Liz nervously picked at her shirt hem. She plunged ahead, her brown eyes focused on Jay's face, not wavering. "I'm not saying that I think you're a dangerous man, Jay. I just don't know you. And I think I'm not in a great period in my life right now to trust my judgment." Liz slowly leaned back against the sofa, spent from the telling of her story.

She was going to be brutally honest so he would know not to waste his time with her. "Truth is Jay, I think you're a decent man. You're good to Ben. I know he'll be sorry he missed you tonight. But you scare the proverbial hell out of me by just coming around."

"Why?" he asked, puzzled by her confession.

She sat up suddenly. "Because," she said, sounding like a bullet ricocheting off a steel wall, "I'm thirty-four years old and I have three kids. The protective membrane I thought Mike and I were building for each other and our family was in reality a disintegrating shell. And I didn't notice."

Liz went on as if to herself. "I guess I was the only one who wanted that shell to hold the good in and the bad out. So now," she said, looking at Jay, "I look around and ask myself is anything real? How can I tell what's real?"

She turned her head away, fighting to hold herself together. With a dry chuckle and a "well you asked" look, Liz finished. "Not exactly a festive aura tonight, is it?"

Good Lord, Liz Daniels. He stopped by for a little flirt and you make everything so sky-is-falling serious. The next set of commercial jingles began, filling the silence. Now she expected he would leave and that would be that.

Jay cleared his throat. He spoke evenly, like they were talking about the weather, but his eyes were sharp with attention. "I get the part about the relationship where you say the coating, the armor that was supposed to provide the special place for you didn't really exist. I've seen that in some friends' lives and I guess that's one of the reasons I haven't gotten married. The women I dated didn't seem to want what I wanted and they weren't who I could see myself being content with for very long, so we didn't even get close to the altar."

Liz found herself leaning forward to better focus on his words.

"The one woman I thought I was close to," he went on, "didn't care so much for regular people. She only liked the special ones, the important ones. She liked my clients and their stature a heck of a lot more than me." He shook his head at this and stood.

"If you're searching for a particular quality in people, Liz, you either find it or you don't. Hopefully the same type of people get lined up with one another. My brother always says he hopes the jerks end up with one another or God help us all!" He laughed aloud at this, then offered Liz his hand.

When she hesitated, he chuckled. "I don't bite, Liz." He pulled her to her feet. "And I don't lie so I'll tell you the truth right now. I won't push you, but I would like to spend some time with you."

She started to shake her head but he stopped her, his hand still holding hers. "I can appreciate your need for space and I'll give you that. I'm not asking for anything except that we get to know each other."

He dropped her hand and ran his fingers through his hair, glancing at a loud noise from the TV show.

"When I decided I didn't want to live in any more cities near any more strangers this was where I knew I wanted to go. Home. I guess you could say I've come to Benton to make of my life what I couldn't elsewhere. And it looks like you're doing the same."

Jay walked toward the kitchen, picking up empty popcorn bowls as he went. When he got to the doorway, he looked at her over his shoulder. She was standing by the sofa, Tess now asleep on the floor.

"I promise I won't hassle you. But if you don't mind, I could use a little help finding the dish soap." His self-assured, easy going behavior did it. She snapped.

"You don't get it," Liz said between her teeth. "I'm not ready for another relationship. Maybe never." Old memories, hurtful, painful stuff, had been resurrected this evening and he was to blame.

"I get it, Liz," Jay said gently. "I just think it's ridiculous to say you're not ready for another relationship until you find out what kind of one we're talking about. Didn't ask you to marry me, darlin', just asked where you keep your damn soap." He was grinning but a challenge was evident under his easy going manner.

She stared at him, then smiled despite herself. Walking to the doorway, Liz pointed at the cupboard under the kitchen sink.

"See?" he said. "Sometimes it's just one step here, one step there, and see where it takes you."

෩෩෩

Liz was digging in dirt again. This time she was thinning some old plantings at the McNeary place on the south edge of Benton. Ben, Jane and Tess were now into their fourth week of school.

It was a real pleasure for Liz to be able to do things well again. She could throw herself into work and still have time with her kids. Having her baby start school hadn't been a traumatic event but rather another celebration in their family. Still, in the back of her mind was always the thought: when would the next storm cloud the horizon and screw up everything?

A clod of dirt landed near her feet. "Had a break yet?" Jay asked as he came to stand beside her bent figure.

"No, I haven't but I've got quite a bit to do, yet," she replied, hands deep in the soil.

He watched her work. "I've been checking pastures, putting out salt and mineral. Thought I'd take a break, see what you were doing."

She was pleased by this, and immediately scared by her reaction. Maybe to fill in the silence as much as anything, she asked if he knew of the house with the red door about a mile north of town.

"I'm thinking about renting it and fixing it up with paint and wallpaper and maybe a hammer. Do you think it would be worth the trouble?"

Jay didn't answer right away, giving her time to worry she'd been too impulsive. Liz rocked back on her heels and looked up at him, his face framed by the brim of his hat and the hot summer sky.

"I'd say it's definitely worth the effort," he finally answered. "The foundation's good and the house has only been empty a few months. It doesn't take long for an old house to fall into disrepair but this one has always been well taken care of so I think it would be fine. Have you thought this through, Liz?" He could tell his question annoyed her. He smiled as he added, "it would be a little more inconvenient for you and your kids."

"Actually I have thought it through," she said brusquely. "It will be fine for them to ride their bikes into town or take the bus. Besides, I like the space, the quiet. All that room," she gestured at the sky. She then returned to her digging with renewed energy, sorry she'd brought it up.

"I know who owns it and I bet they'd rent it to you," Jay offered. "They probably won't ask for too much in return for someone living there and taking care of it. If you'd like, I'll look into it for you."

"Thank you," she said and reached for a plant. He would have offered to help with her move if things worked out, but her silence irked him.

Instead, he said he'd check with the owners and let her know. Jay drove off to finish his afternoon's work. She dug her way through the old bulb stand.

The owners, Jay told her the next morning after the kids and Annie left for school, would be pleased to have a new renter. They shot him a price and agreed to provide whatever materials she might need. Liz looked up while wiping off the kitchen table.

"Who owns it?" She finished the table and offered him some coffee. She was relieved when he turned her down. Jay, dressed in a forest green shirt and khaki slacks, was obviously on his way to somewhere other than the pasture.

"I've got to get going this morning. I'm heading off to a meeting in Kearney with some people on a new office complex."

Her hand slowed as she wiped crumbs off of the counter. "I thought you were doing odd jobs at a ranch while you were fixing up that house of your grandparents."

"I am," he said. "But I'm also trying to establish my business closer to home, not travel so much, and this would be a good start."

"Well, best of luck then," Liz said, tilting her head toward him.

He handed her two gold keys on a ring. "Here's the key to the house. Get whatever you need at Mac's Hardware and charge it. And Liz, would you do something for me?" he said as he opened the door.

"What?"

He noticed she was careful about how far she extended herself and grinned at this. "Would you tell Ben to lay low for a couple days? I won't be working on the house for a while."

He was back in his pickup and driving down the street when she realized she still didn't know the owner's name. She glanced at her watch. She'd get the name later.

Right now she had a couple hours before she needed to be at the Dirt Store. Time enough to check out the house and make herself some notes before heading to work. Over her lunch hour she could pick up whatever she needed at Mac's and start cleaning after work.

&⁂&

"Mr. Robbins," bank president John Daly spoke for the group, "this is an impressive port-folio. Very impressive." The meeting room at Kearney National was traditional bank fare.

Dark oak, gleaming and powerful, filled the richly carpeted and draped room. Large, important chairs surrounded the even larger and more important oval conference table. Good lighting and a coffee and soda bar comple-mented the room.

A grandfather clock measured spent time as the four businessmen studied Jay's work on the easels and spread out before them on the table.

Daly continued. "What I'm most interested in knowing is what your thoughts are on this project and what kind of time frame we're look-ing at here." They had already looked over Jay's portfolio and letters of recommendation.

Frank Miggington, owner of a large regional accounting firm, added, "And I want to know whether or not you think you can provide the kind of design that will draw the attention and clients we're after."

Daly and Miggington were in charge. J.R. Chourney and Stan Vondrak, though fellow investors, were silent partners in the meeting as well as the venture itself.

All eyes were on Jay as he worked his way through their questions. "Based on what you've told me, the purpose of this site, and the kind of design work I've done in the past, I can tell you three things."

Jay moved from the main presentation easel to rest his tanned forearms on the back of a chair near the group. "One, Kearney is the kind of community that will reward this type of project. Look at the restaurants, clothing stores, medical community; the entire infrastructure. Kearney has what it takes to financially support a professional building of this type. Two," he continued, moving nearer the power hub of Miggington and Daly, "Can I design the right look and the best function possible in the space you want? In a word, yes."

He let that sink in. Years of experience and climbing from assistant to principal on jobs had taught him to trust his work and not hesitate to show his confidence.

"Three? What you really want to know is do I understand the people and the professionals in this region well enough to bring a big city look to Kearney and align it with the heartland images we see all around us?"

He paused, looking each of them in the eye. "I do and I can." He let this statement stand. "You're welcome to contact the people I worked with on any of these projects and to ask any questions you like. I'm available right now so if you're ready, I'm ready." He began gathering his materials, then stopped and spoke directly to Daly.

"We all need to be heading in the same direction before we start, if we start. I would need to know who's my direct line of contact. The only way to undertake a project like this is to know who's ultimately in charge and what's the line of communication."

He didn't wait long. His first thought after an initial rush of satisfaction was that he'd have less time for Ben and their project, and the boy's mother and their fumbling start.

ℰ☯ℛ

Liz opened the red door with one of the keys Jay had given her and entered the house with pleasure, the lock had worked smoothly. She glanced around the mud room and in at the kitchen full of appliances.

Walking through the combination living and dining room, a large dining room table and chairs were already there. On to the first floor bedroom with its own bathroom and walk-in closet. Back through the living room and up the old oak staircase. Brushing her hand along the worn but polished hand rail, Liz climbed to the two loft bedrooms with the shared bathroom.

In Benton

Down again through the mud room to the basement storage and furnace rooms. Back to the main floor, noticing the freezer, and through the back of the kitchen to the laundry area and the food pantry.

Nothing needed to be done here. No wallpaper torn, no paint flaking, no mess on the floor, and no light bulbs to replace. The staircase and lofts were beautiful. The house had to be a hundred years old. Everything was clean and in perfect repair. Why wasn't anyone living here? she asked herself. Then she noticed the hum of the refrigerator. She stared at it, then slowly reached for the door handle. Inside was a bottle of wine with a note tied to it's cork. Five cold stemmed glasses sat beside it.

She took the note off and leaned against the counter as she read the handwritten scrawl.

Liz,
    Hope this place will work for all of you. Should get back to town in time to meet you out here around 6:30 if that's all right. I'll bring supper and help you celebrate your new home.
        Jay

If that's all right, she thought angrily. He's bringing supper and he's not waiting for an answer, is he? I don't want this. I just want the damn house. Now something was owed.

But Jay hadn't asked anything except for her friendship, she argued with herself. Ah, but Liz, you know better than that. There's no free lunch.

These things have strings. No, he's not like that. He's been kind to Ben.

She had inklings of the kind of man he was, but she'd had similar insights into Mike and been dismally wrong. Or he had steered her wrong by not sharing who and what he really was, letting her believe her opinion, and for that she could not forgive him. She'd taken a several year detour with Mike. She didn't have time or the energy for another wrong turn.

What was it her mother had said when she was a teenager? They would be having one of their wonderful after-school conversations, talking about her studies and friends and the guys in her class. Mom had always said that it just took a little more time to be sure of someone. It didn't take years, like someone young often thought was being asked. Only a little more time before it was too late to turn down another road.

There's no such thing as a permanent mistake, Mom would add, any more than there's a permanent right move. The only really permanent thing in life is your will to conquer your problems and move forward with integrity and grit. And love. Always love.

Yes, Mom, but it's so easy to say, "Take your time, think it through, don't make a move without being careful." Where does your heart enter in when everything is so calculated?

Liz had asked this one day when she was home for her first fall break from college. She'd been dating a boy in her History of the Americas class. Her heart missed several beats a minute when he was near.

"Honey," her mom had said, "there is nothing more fabulous and exciting than love. At any age. All I'm saying is sometimes people, including older people, get chemistry mixed up with love that's really good for them. I married your dad less than four months after I met him and I know my folks were concerned. But I got to know the inner person, the place where he was real with me and I was real with him. And we liked that part of each other. If you just take a little time, way will show."

Liz shrugged off the long ago conversation, wary of the thoughts a simple bottle of wine had evoked. She could get through this evening because he did her a nice turn. Then she would let him know, once and for all, she wasn't interested.

Quit standing around, Liz, and get to work. You've found yourself a new home, and even if this isn't the nice, uncomplicated way you wanted to go about it, buck up.

When she arrived back at the store she asked Arch if she could quit early and borrow his pickup. Then she looked up Annie at the school and enlisted her aid and that of a couple more teachers for help in moving after school let out.

Ben saw the note on the fridge door as he reached for a yogurt. "Jay's gone today. You've got the day off. Love, Mom." He took more time with his after school snack than normal, digging for some crumbled cookies at the bottom of the cookie jar.

"Hey, Jane, want to work on that tree house out back?" Ben asked.

She looked up from her juice box. "Aren't you going to Jay's?"

"Nah. I thought we could put up a swing and maybe find a ladder somewhere." Through the kitchen window Ben saw the Dirt Store pickup backing up to the porch. Two teachers jumped out of the back and a moment later his band instructor Jason White walked into the kitchen, surprising Ben into an uncustomary silence.

"Hi, Ben. Ready for the move?"

"I found a place for us," Liz announced as she, Annie, and Vern Braithwaite followed Jason in the door. "It's right outside of town and we're moving in today. I've already moved the odds and ends from storage."

Everyone helped carry out clothes on hangers and the house plants from Minneapolis. Then the adults picked up the bedroom furniture and a few chairs from storage. They had the bedrooms set up by six o'clock.

Waving her thanks as the pickup drove off, Liz turned to her kids and smiled. Stepping closer to the railing, she finally noticed the view from their front porch. Blooming goldenrod was dancing in the light breeze. Yellowish brown meadow larks sang their hauntingly poetic verses from the fence lines and power poles near the driveway.

Across the road, cows and their calves grazed side by side, moving in the same direction as if on cue. Now and again a calf would begin bucking and kicking.

Several other calves joined in the rabbit race, tails high in the air as if joyously celebrating the evening. The girls and their mother sat on the porch swing, taking it all in.

ഇന്ദ്ര

"She's been asleep awhile," Ben told Jay. "I think she got tired going up and down the steps. Did you know we got everything moved in? Just finished." Ben was anxious to be the first to show Jay inside the house, especially his loft bedroom.

Jane and Tess had slipped away from the swing and were digging in a sand pile they'd found next to an old garden bed, behind the house.

"Go ahead, Ben. I'll be right in," Jay said, handing two bags to the boy. "Take these into the kitchen for me, would you?"

"Sure. But hurry, okay?"

Liz woke a few minutes later and saw Jay's profile as he sat straddling the porch railing, eyes on the distant hilled pastures. At her stirring, he turned.

"Ben said you had a big day. Thought I'd give you a few more minutes." He watched her blink, then smother a yawn. "So you got it in your head to move right away."

"You could have told me this place didn't need a single thing done to it." She pushed herself up into a sitting position. "It's even been cleaned recently. What's going on?"

He reached over and took her hands. Swinging his leg over the railing, Jay pulled her up and walked her to the door. "Let's just eat, okay? I brought some Chinese from Kearney and the wine's non-alcoholic. I didn't want to leave anyone out so I found a bottle of apple cider, fizzed."

She would have to wait for some answers. What with the kids wound tight from both the move and their new surroundings, it was a loud supper. Liz had to admit Jay had hit the jackpot with supper. They all loved Chinese.

After the meal, Ben and Jane ran outside to explore the barn while Tess returned to the sand pile. Paper plates gathered and trashed, the adults moved into the living room.

"That was wonderful. Thank you," Jay said from the sofa.

Liz sat in front of the hearth, her head swinging around at his words. "It's I who should be thanking you. You arranged for this place and brought supper. Clearly you have a larger hand in all of this than I understand right now. I would like to understand." Eyebrow raised, she waited.

"Well, thank you for sharing your family with me tonight is what I meant to say. That was like the old days with my family. As for whose place this is, well, this is my family's place."

Liz had decided it would be something like that. She didn't immediately react, though he'd expected her to do so.

He'd thought she would resent what might look like encroachment on his part. "My parents, brother, sister and I used to live here. Several years ago I updated the inside for my folks when I was in between projects."

He surveyed the room. "About five years ago Mom and Dad were in a car accident on their way back from a livestock show in Denver. Both were killed. My brother didn't need this place since he and his wife already had a home on another part of the ranch. My sister Lisa lives in Kearney with her husband and family. So we rented it out to a teacher whenever a new one came to town. Last spring after our last renter moved out we decided to leave it empty."

"Why didn't you say something?" She tried to keep her voice neutral. She probably failed as his voice was heated when he replied.

"If I'd told you what would you have done?" he asked, appraising her intently. "As far as I'm concerned this is a business arrangement. I talked with my brother and his wife last night and they were happy to rent it out to a family again. They're going to be home tonight if you want to meet them. If not, you can do it another time."

She stood her ground. "What about the rent? For such a nice home it seems a little low, even for a little town like Benton."

"It's fine. We've always just rented it out to help with the taxes. Mainly, we wanted someone here to keep the place alive. If you want, Kent could come over and till the garden next spring. He usually does that when he's doing his own."

She sat still, torn between the clawing feeling of being trapped and the desire to stay in this lovely space. Liz looked out the dining room window to the hills beyond the backyard for one heart beat, two heart beats, three.

"I would like a garden. And I wouldn't mind taking care of a lawn."

"Liz." He waited for her to look at him. "You owe me nothing. I think you've got a lot of guts. It would be more than a little tough to move here, to adjust to our customs. I admire that."

Breathe in and out, she told herself. Calm. There is no trap here. "Well," she said steadily, "I suppose we'd better go meet the rest of the landlords before it gets any later." Liz strode out of the room, calling for her three to head for the car.

She had taken several steps toward the mud room door before he answered, "Sure, bring the kids along. They'll have a blast." And of course the kids already knew each other from school.

ℰℭ

Kyle Robbins, a year older than Ben, was his frequent rival for recess quarterback. Fran was in Jane's class and little Patrick was three and a half, and a ham.

Their parents walked up from behind a large metal outbuilding toward the commotion stirred up by the arrival of the Daniels family and Jay.

Liz recognized the woman she'd seen with Jay in the pickup and at the park. The kids piled out of the back seat and were greeted by a bounding gray and black dog with a long fan tail.

"Don't worry about her," Kent called. "She tries for the ferocious look but she wouldn't hurt a flea," he said as they drew closer. He was a slightly older version of Jay with the same strong, handsome features and challenging grin.

He and Bonnie greeted Jay and were introduced to Liz with a "Bonnie, Kent, this is Liz. And these are her kids. Ben and Tess over there with Kyle, Jane next to Fran. And this little guy, Liz," he reached down to pick up the little boy straining for attention and tossed him in the air above him, "this is my buddy Patrick. How's that arm doing?"

"It's okay, Uncle Jay," Patrick hollered over his shoulder as he ran off to join the older kids already starting up a game.

Bonnie and Liz strolled over to admire several perennial flower beds in their fall glory. "I remember seeing you a time or two with Jay," Liz began.

Bonnie nodded. "He's good to ask me if I want to go along and get some groceries when he's driving to town. The kids are always begging him to stop by the park and play with them."

Dressed in faded jeans and an old sweatshirt with University of Benton written across the front, Bonnie had her dark hair pulled back in a simple ponytail. She looked more like a recent graduate than a mother of three.

They sized each other up, their talk turning to kids, the surrounding shopping area, and their favorite books. Liz felt herself relax during her visit with Bonnie. It wasn't so much what they talked about as how quickly they got to the meat of a subject.

Leaning against Liz's Toyota, Kent and Jay discussed the area news, fall cattle prices, and the harvest soon to be underway. Kent had heard in town that McMeens were selling out this winter. Bob McMeen was going to haul his cows to the sale barn after the corn harvest and rent out his land to one of the larger farmers in the area.

Jay asked about Kent's calves. "Will you keep them and feed 'em 'til after the new year?"

"I don't know what to do," his brother replied with a deep sigh. "Every time the cattle and grain markets get this depressed I think I know what to do based on the last time. Seems like I'm always wrong."

"Remember Dad going through this? He'd say he didn't know what to do," Jay reminded Kent, "but he remembered the same conversation with his dad. Doesn't get any easier, does it?"

Kent shook his head, using his boot toe to nudge the gravel at his feet. "You'd think with market analysis and newsletters, the Packers and Stockyards Act, all these cattle associations, and the Board..."

"What the hell do a bunch of suits in Chicago know about cattle?" Jay interrupted his brother, heating up at the mention of the Chicago Board of Trade. "They take a piece of paper and trade it. It's squat to them what that does to our family's livelihood."

Boiling now, Jay's voice rose. "Wouldn't you love just once to trade on some national newscaster guy's job? Put his wages on the Board of

Trade and have people come in every day and tell him what he's worth that day or the next?"

"Oh well, today there are too many newscasters in Los Angeles so your wages drop eight percent. Or, it rained in Indiana and Ohio today so your wages, even though you're working in Los Angeles, are in the toilet because we can't have any news today in the Ohio Valley. Jesus Christ! What's the matter with us? What other industry would allow that kind of control of their business and call it progress? As for the government farm programs and the so-called Ag banks and the Department of Agriculture..."

Liz caught the tail end of the animated conversation as the women strolled back to the car.

"I guess you can't ever really get the ranching bug out of your blood," Jay said by way of explanation.

"Why would you want to?" she asked, surprising him with both her comment and her calm interest.

He studied her silently for a moment. "I guess I always hated the lousy financial deal we got in this business so I took the chicken way out and got me a real job." This for Kent's benefit.

Kent took the bait. "Probably ninety percent of the men, especially young guys, still out here wish they were in someone else's shoes. Except," he said, gently tugging on one of the belt loops on Bonnie's jeans, pulling her against him. "When you get up in the morning and really see the sunrise. Or when we lay in bed at night, exhausted, and we both still love where we live and what we do. I suppose those are the payoffs," he said, seriously, "'cause they sure as hell aren't in the paycheck."

Kent studied Liz, his eyes twinkling. "I'm glad to hear you've moved into our old place. I couldn't understand why Jay wanted it left vacant after Bob Shickley moved out the end of school last spring. Now I get it." Liz felt warmth move up her neck.

"If I'd known you were going to hassle Liz, I wouldn't have brought her over here," Jay retorted.

"Who says I'm hassling her?" Kent countered with enthusiasm. "Just saying I now understand."

"All right the two of you, that's enough," Bonnie said, tired from a long day. She had stepped between them. "You'll have Liz thinking we're backward idiots living out here in the sticks." She turned to Liz. "Would you like to come in and join us for supper? We were out back checking on a couple calves and hadn't gotten in to eat yet."

"Thanks, Bonnie, but we just finished. Please, I don't want to keep you from your meal." Five minutes later they were driving back toward the house she had begun to call the Red Door. As soon as the car was parked, Ben and Jane jumped out and headed to their new rooms. Tess followed more slowly, glad tomorrow was Saturday.

Standing beside her car door Liz turned to Jay "You purposefully didn't rent this place out to see if I might want it?"

"Kent didn't need to say that."

She waited, eyes steady, listening for a lie.

"Look, I told you I'm the guy without a date for the dance because I want to take you. Besides, this place means something to us so we don't rent it out lightly."

She shut her car door and walked up the steps, stopping on the porch to look back at him. "It's going to work great for us. The way you remodeled it and still left its past is wonderful." He was still watching her from the side of her car as she reached for the door.

"Don't do this anymore, Jay," she said, choosing her next words carefully. "Don't be so nice to me. I'm not interested in any kind of relationship at all." She went in and shut the door quietly behind her.

He started after her, then thought better of it, and climbed in his pickup to drive back to town.

Ⅎ⇛

A week later, Bonnie stopped in the Dirt Store and found Liz working in the back room. "Mind if I bother you?"

"You're no bother. What's up?"

"I want to ask a favor of you. Please tell me if you'd rather not, okay?" Bonnie leaned back against a work bench, watching Liz scrub her hands. "I'm thinking of taking on a second part-time job, this one on Saturdays. Most of the time Kent and I will work it out so he'll be around, but once in a while I'll need someone for the kids to call if they need something."

"I'd be glad to help you out. They're welcome to come over, Bonnie, for that matter. My kids would love it. What kind of job? I know you already drive our school bus route."

"With prices as bad as they are, both crops and cattle, I need to dig in deeper and help with the cash flow so we can ride this thing out. I'm more than a little afraid that a lot of us aren't going to make it, no matter what we do." She bit her lip.

"Anyway," she went on, "the post office is interviewing for a substitute rural delivery position. I took the exam and did pretty well. The pay would be good and so would the insurance. I suppose that's the main reason I'm looking into this job, the benefits."

She waited for Liz's response. It came immediately. "Just count on me whenever you need me."

"Thanks, Liz. I appreciate it. I could repay you in kind, if you'd like. Now that my brother-in-law and you are seeing eye to eye you may need some evening child care, eh?" She touched Liz's arm as she turned to leave.

"Bonnie, wait."

Bonnie looked at Liz expectantly.

"Jay and I aren't exactly seeing eye to eye."

"Oh," Bonnie said slowly. "I thought you two were interested in one another."

"Um, he's interested. I'm not."

Bonnie considered Liz's answer, then asked if she had time for a cup of coffee. They walked down the street to the Mustang Café and settled in a back booth.

"Did Jay say something that has you mad at him?" Bonnie began. "Because I know what he can be like sometimes. Pushy, bull headed, a Robbins." She laughed as she said this, as if it was to be expected.

Her brevity was refreshing. Liz swallowed some coffee and shook her head. "No. I'm not mad at him. It's nothing like that. I barely know him. I'm just not interested in seeing anyone."

"Mind if I ask why?"

Liz stared at her, now unnerved by her directness. "I...um...I'm not sure what to say. I feel a little strange talking about this with his sister-in-law, to be truthful, Bonnie." Bonnie laughed, reached for her coffee cup, and leveled a knowing look at Liz.

"Well I just thought, oh, never mind," Bonnie said.

"Thought what?"

"I guess I misjudged what I saw at our place last week on your part, that's all." Bonnie changed the subject. Liz's face said all Bonnie needed to hear.

✧

The weather over the next few days was golden. Balmy, sunny days began and ended with cool mornings and evenings. Sunrises were so pure even the town grousers took note. Sunsets were photographed by many a local. Breezes and birds and grasses; all seemed to be changing, adjusting to the new season.

Glorious fall hit Benton full force and nearly everyone was caught up in its magic. School had been in session for some time and now the temperature was matching the season. Sweater weather had arrived and Liz suspected her favorite time of the year would be even better this year.

Ben missed his close contact with Jay. He invented ways to skip the bus and show up for a while. Then Jay would give him a ride home or Liz would stop to pick him up after she got off work.

"Hello? Oh, Darlene. Yes, I'm about to head out to work. No, they've already left for school. Tomorrow? Yes, I will. Oh? Well, it's pretty easy, actually. You take Highway 35 north from Kearney about an hour and a half. Benton is right off the highway. We're about another mile north of town. Just stay on the main street and go past the bank and the swimming pool. The house has a red door. Yes, very distinctive. About three? All right. Goodbye."

The cordless phone clattered on the kitchen counter. Staring at her chaotic household, she leaned on the counter and shook with uncontrollable laughter. Oh well, Liz thought as she wiped her eyes, breathing in deeply. It could be immaculate and still not pass the test. Darlene wasn't one that could be satisfied, after all.

Mike's mother had never taken a shine to Liz. Darlene had trotted her around in front of those she'd wanted to impress when Mike and she were first married, dropping tidbits about her career successes.

After the newness wore off, so had Liz's allure. Then Darlene pretty much bothered her daughter until Ben was born. Darlene's perfect mothering kicked in at that point and nothing, absolutely nothing Liz did or said was right.

Liz came to understand this was nothing personal. But that didn't lessen the pain of the many run-ins Liz had with her mother-in-law over what were, when reduced to their most basic form, simply the desire of one human being to control another.

Finally Liz caught on that this was just how Darlene dealt with her own self doubts. She'd always felt bad about Ron Daniels. Mike's dad had seemed like a good kind of guy. But he steered clear of Darlene, throwing himself ever harder into his work and his golf game.

"I've felt sorry for her for years now. But that doesn't mean I'm looking forward to her visit." Liz had talked Annie into a quick lunch, hoping for a sympathetic ear.

Annie reached over and grasped her firmly. "Liz. Friend. You'll be fine." She stood up and gathered up the bill and her purse. Lowering her voice to a stage whisper, she leaned toward Liz. "Just don't let her get under your skin. Plan a house fire for an hour after she arrives and she'll leave in a flash!" Laughing, she headed back to English 9 and a lesson on point of view.

Easy for you to say, Liz thought. I'd better get busy until the appointed hour. Why today? Of all days why would Darlene show up in Benton today?

A week ago Jay had asked her to go to Kearney with him for a dinner meeting. He'd driven Ben home and had stayed a few minutes to visit with Liz. The men from the office project wanted to sign contracts and toast the beginning of their business association.

She accepted the invitation, knowing that even with the others present this would indeed be a date. She was determined to have an enjoyable dinner, thank Jay for his kindnesses to Ben, and return to her quiet life.

She'd decided on the right dress, a sleek burgundy cocktail dress. And now Darlene. Surely she could spend time with Darlene and then go on about her day without the visit affecting her. Even Mike's arrival would not fluster her like this. Liz was going to need several distractions before three.

Liz's resolve vanished with Darlene's look at the door. Never one to speak directly, she commented on the quaint porch and the amount of dust on her rental car and Liz got the gist. She had lowered herself yet another rung and was now a country simpleton.

No matter the grandchildren were happy and she was rebuilding her life. Darlene's dear son had been left adrift and her ex-daughter-in-law was to blame.

Liz wondered where those open minded in-laws were who were featured in supermarket magazines. The ones who saw the holes in their own child and still professed love and support for all concerned.

Liz had endured a stilted half hour conversation with Darlene by the time the kids arrived home on the bus. She had debated what to say about Darlene's impending arrival and finally opted to simply tell her children that their grandmother was coming for a brief visit.

Flying in from Minneapolis, staying a little while, complaining about her welcome, that was Darlene's way. The kids had seen enough of her role in their family's life to give her wide berth. Instinctively they had become careful in their contact and, of course, Darlene blamed Liz.

The kids showed Darlene their rooms and the barn and sheds outside. She stepped around the weeds and listened politely to their chatter. Then they moved inside once more to drink ice tea and visit about school. Liz followed along.

At five o'clock Darlene looked pointedly at her watch and stood, smoothing her tasteful skirt. "Well, I suppose I'd better be going. I just wanted to come see my grandchildren since they live so far away from Grandmother now. You really should rethink this, Liz."

Their eyes met above Ben's head.

For once Liz simply returned the look, keeping her heart beat steady. "Rethink what, Darlene?"

"This." She gestured around the room. Darlene's ringed hand mocked the life they were building in Benton. "I realize you are taking a little...side trip to recover from your failed marriage. But do you really think it's in the children's best interest to end up here, in this little spot on a dirt trail, for heaven's sake?"

Darlene's voice took on a coaxing vein. "Think of them for once. You could still live in Minneapolis. After all, it's a big place. You wouldn't have to run into Mike and his new friend. You have a real job there and I could have my grandchildren."

Liz knew it was no use arguing. Darlene would never understand why Liz had made this choice nor would she care to truly listen. Her stated concern for her grandchildren came nowhere close to what she wanted. The whole world rotated around Darlene's axis, or so she thought.

Darlene left shortly afterward. The kids gave her compulsory hugs and she drove off, back to the airport in Kearney. Back to her beautifully appointed house with large closets and everything in its place, and out of Liz's hair.

By six-thirty the hot shower and tall glass of grapefruit juice were working. Her private venting was winding down and she was no longer talking back to herself.

Liz was putting in her earrings when Tess shouted she could see Jay's pickup from her bedroom window. Picking up her black beaded jacket, Liz met Jay, who was dressed in slacks and a sports jacket, at the porch.

"Ready?" He couldn't take his eyes off her.

"I am. Just a second while I say goodbye to the kids and Janet." She handed a slip of paper to the teenager Annie had suggested. On it was the phone number of the restaurant where she could be reached and a couple emergency numbers, just in case.

After quick kisses and promises of good behavior, Liz walked down the steps. Jay opened her pickup door and shut it behind her.

He walked around and climbed into his seat. As he turned on the ignition, he turned to Liz, a smile tugging at the corners of his mouth. "You look beautiful. I wasn't certain you'd agree to go out tonight, but I sure am glad you did."

They drove through Benton and down the highway to Kearney, making small talk about the harvest and weather, work at the Dirt Store and the remodeling job.

They arrived at The Far Lodge a few minutes before eight and joined the partners at a secluded round table. Liz was seated next to Stan Morely. Jay sat next to Liz and John Daly. A cocktail waitress soon came to take their orders.

When the drinks arrived, J.R. Chourney asked Jay about the availability of materials he was planning to use. Frank Miggington and Stan engaged Liz in a conversation about the Minneapolis business center.

Seconds were ordered by Stan and J.R. and everyone settled in to study the menu. When the waiter arrived, they ordered various steak and seafood dinners.

Liz excused herself and Jay pulled her chair back as she left for the restroom. Stan spoke up almost immediately after she was gone. "That's quite the woman you've got there, Jay. Are you two an item?"

Irritated by Stan's question, Jay changed the subject. "Actually, Liz and I haven't known one another all that long. Now gentlemen, should we take a look at those contracts and get them out of the way before our food arrives?"

Jay had already studied a faxed copy of the contract, so he looked through the pages, checking that his key points were covered and nothing new had been inserted. Jay signed the copies and passed them to his right.

Liz returned midway through the business deal. She watched the men, gauging the leadership among them. When they were done, each man took a copy. Jay smiled at Liz and reached for his drink. He tapped his glass to hers and lifted it in the air to give a toast: "To our office complex. May it be everything we hope for and more."

The Far Lodge was nearly full, Liz noticed. Near her a couple was deep in conversation, unaware of their surroundings. Good site for a business or social meal, she mused, with its private seating areas and soft music.

Soon the food arrived. The waiter efficiently served each person, making pleasant talk as he worked. Taking another drink order, he left.

Jay smiled at Liz as he reached for his fork, noticing her blank expression. He leaned forward, trying to get her to make eye contact, but she merely nodded and picked up her fork. Jay spoke to John about a meeting the following week, then turned back to her, noticing that she was in a hushed conversation with Stan.

Suddenly she pushed sharply back from the table, her chair scraping on the floor. Liz said a few terse words to her left, then turned to Jay and apologized as she reached behind her for her jacket. "I'm sorry about this, Jay." To the group at the table she said, "I'm afraid I must excuse myself" before she stood and walked out of the restaurant.

Pacing outside, Liz struggled for composure. She pulled on her jacket but could still feel the night's chill. There had even been some talk of snow in the long term forecast.

She laughed ruefully, thinking how living in a rural community had put talk of weather alongside *hi, how are you?* in her daily conversational rituals. But that, in there, had nothing to do with rural lifestyle. And it was inexcusable.

Noticing a bookstore next door with lights still on, Liz walked across the Lodge's parking lot and went in to warm herself. Shortly after her arrival, the door jingled another customer's entrance. She saw Jay's shoes before he sat beside her on the reading sofa.

"So what's new?" he nodded at the newspaper in her hands.

"Just the usual," she answered, her voice clipped. "Murder, political maneuvering, he-said-she-said stuff." She took a deep breath. "Stan came on to me, big time."

Jay nodded, his jaw clamped tight. Eyes like a hawk scanning the terrain, he said he'd figured that was what had happened. "I guess the others figured it out, too."

"I'm sorry..." she began.

"What the hell do you have to be sorry for?" he said with rancor.

She tapped his arm lightly, waiting for him to listen to her. "I was saying, I'm sorry I had to walk out like that but it was either a graceful exit or a black eye to my dinner neighbor and that wouldn't have looked too cool. I hope this won't hurt your deal. What a Rick!" she added under her breath.

"A what?"

She let go a short sigh. "Years ago when I was new in the business, I was assigned to work with a guy named Rick. Ol' Rick came on to me while we were touring the job at his company. He talked real soft and it was hard to hear what he said, but it was basically pretty low-life "talk". I didn't want to cause a scene so I simply walked away. That, he took for encouragement. I had a heck of a time keeping space between us the rest of the job. I decided afterward that if a similar situation ever came up, I'd deal with it differently."

She put the newspaper back on the table and tucked a wisp of hair behind her ear. "Unfortunately, I've had to deal with similar situations a few times."

She hesitated, then laid her hand on his. "Just accept it, Jay. You and me? It's not going to work. I'm just not ready for a romantic relationship with anyone right now. Maybe never. And I want to be honest with you about that."

Jay frowned but he spoke calmly, taking her hand in his before she thought to move it. "Listen, I'm the one who's sorry. I didn't know Stan very well or I wouldn't have put you in that position. After you left though, it was apparent that the others do, because they tore into him. Not all men are that way, or look the other way. He took off out the back door."

She looked down at her hand in his as he went on.

"And about the other? You can ask anyone. I'm not very good at accepting something I don't want to accept." He stood up, pulling her along with him. They were outside now, walking toward his pickup. "So what did he say?"

In a detached sort of way she admired his handling of her earlier statement. "I took his first lewd comment in stride," she answered. "Figured he'd tire of his game and knock it off," she answered. "But then he slipped his hand onto my leg and that was it."

Jay opened the pickup door, still holding her hand.

"You're ignoring what I said in there," she pointed out.

"No, just walking around it," he answered honestly, waiting for her to step into his pickup.

A small smile formed on her lips. "Same thing." She tilted her head back, sizing him up. "You would be really good at political spin, you know; ignore what you want to ignore, emphasize what you want center staged."

He grinned back. "You hungry?" he asked as he again gestured for her to get in.

John Daly appeared around the front of the cab. "Liz, please accept my apologies for this evening. I am very sorry this happened. Embarrassed actually." He held out his hand to her and she took it in a firm handshake.

"Forget it, John," Liz said. "I don't want this to be an uncomfortable situation for any of you." Jay and John shook hands and after agreeing to meet early Tuesday morning at the bank, John left.

Liz and Jay drove to a popular seafood place nearby where they dined on broiled salmon and crab Alfredo and kept their conversation light.

Later they sat on the Red Door's porch swing, bundled in coats, sipping coffee and listening to a station out of Chihuahua. "If I hadn't run into an old acquaintance of yours today I'd still have been impressed with your handling of 'Rick' tonight," Jay commented.

Liz froze. You've got to be kidding, she told herself. What are the odds?

"And you know? I think that flat tire was the last straw for your mother-in-law, too."

"You didn't really run into Darlene, did you?" How else could he have known she was here? Annie?

He nodded, tapping his boot on the porch floor in time to the music. "She saw me working on the outside of the house. I'm doing the upstairs window trim now. It's really coming along."

She gave him a withering look, impatient now to hear the story she wished hadn't happened.

Chuckling softly, he leaned back in the swing, his arm along the backrest. "Anyway, she kind of just stood there like I should drop my little unimportant job and hustle on over to see what I could do for her."

"That was definitely Darlene," she stated dryly.

Jay laughed again. He sauntered over to the railing and sat back against a column. From her vantage point, Liz could see his face, suddenly serious, as he watched the nearby trees swaying in the breeze. Autumn was hard at work forcing leaves from their summer moorings.

He looked back at her. "You haven't said much about your husband's family but I got the whole load while helping her."

Internally Liz cringed, subconsciously bracing herself. "What did she say?"

"Actually she didn't say too much," Jay responded. "But everything she did say spoke volumes."

He rubbed his hands together to ward off the night chill. "Give me a little credit here, Liz. I've met a few people in my lifetime. Maybe they weren't my ex-in-law but they would have made an interesting run for the title."

Jay grinned again. "She was quite a piece of work," he assured her. "Charmed me into changing the tire and at the same time let me know I wasn't quite in her league. I couldn't help but think how she and my mom were such different people."

A stray tabby, fed for two days and now in danger of becoming the family pet, joined Liz on the swing. Perking up its ears and purring with each stroke of Liz's hand, it appeared to be listening to their conversation.

"Did she mention her visit here today?" she finally asked.

"You mean did she talk about the horrible daughter-in-law with the talons?" He laughed aloud, thoroughly enjoying both the telling of his encounter with Darlene and Liz's need to draw all of it, each uncomfortable detail, out of him.

He drained the last of his coffee. "Actually she seemed to be in a hurry to shake our dust from her fine behind and get back to civilization." He teased her once more. "She looked like a lovely lady, Liz. I'm surprised you two aren't friendly-like."

She sighed slowly. "I feel bad she came so far for a two-hour visit, but that was a really long visit from my perspective. And I'm sorry for Mike and his sister. They do whatever mama says just to keep her off their back. Not everyone sees her that way, of course; she treats everyone differently depending on what she wants."

Liz brushed the cat aside and moved to the railing, sharing Jay's view of the night sky. Stars were everywhere and seemed to be moving ever closer to their vantage point.

"Tell me about your mom," Liz said.

"She'd have died of shame before she ever purposefully or accidentally treated someone like that," he answered softly. "As kids it hurt us to see her get mad at us because we knew she felt worse than we did. People always knew they could count on Mom for help of any kind. She was a fine person."

Liz nodded, her eyes misting a little. "My mom's a lot like that. Dad was away at engineering jobs for weeks at a time. She always said it was like being a military wife without the support network. He only did that for a few years but it was when my sisters and I were young so it had a lasting effect on her. They are a great couple and yet she's fiercely independent. I hope my daughters turn out half as neat as her."

"They will. They've got a neat mom." Jay turned Liz to him and kissed her softly on the lips before saying goodnight.

It was hard to go in from the porch. She reminded herself again, sternly, of the possible pitfalls.

It was hard to drive away. This time he felt things could work out.

❧☙

Liz was out in the yard early the next morning cleaning up dead plants and raking leaves. Arch had given her several of his leftover bulbs and she was scoping for good locations to plant them when a car came tearing up the gravel road, dust billowing out behind it in huge, angry clouds.

She watched its progress. Somebody was in one big hurry, she thought, then recognized the vehicle.

The car braked hard and Liz dropped her rake. Jumping the ditch by the side of the road she ran to the Suburban, immediately catching the driver's frightened look. In the back were all three Robbins kids, their faces a mirror image of their mother's worry.

"Bonnie, what?"

"It's Kent. He was in an accident at the Grayson place. They've been harvesting over there. The hospital called and just said to hurry. Could I leave the kids here?"

"Of course." Liz squeezed Bonnie's hand tightly and hurried to open the rear door. "Come on gang. My kids are around here somewhere."

"Thank you," Bonnie said gratefully, tears filling her eyes. "I'll call as soon as I can." She drove off to Benton's small hospital in search of her husband and some good news.

Liz found busy-work for her kids and Bonnie's. The older kids cleaned the basement while the younger ones tidied the porch. People called asking for news after learning she had the Robbins kids. She'd heard nothing. After spending most of the morning by the phone, she decided to head outside.

She took the children and hiked out into the pasture and picked a bouquet of fall grasses and milkweed pods. Coming upon a large downed limb, Kyle and Ben fashioned a makeshift teeter totter and the children spent an hour in a variety of games and contests on and around it.

On their way back to the Red Door, Kyle moved alongside Liz while the rest of the kids ran ahead. "Do you think my dad's going to be okay?"

Pushing back her own fears, Liz gently took the boy by his shoulders. "I've heard many times that Benton has a good hospital. Your Mom will make sure that everyone does their job. Everything's going to be fine." She hugged him before letting him go.

After he ran off to catch up with the others, she couldn't seem to stop her hands from shaking. Do not make me a liar to that poor boy, God, do you hear me? Don't you dare take his Dad away from him. It was an angry, fearful prayer.

After lunch she put Patrick down for a nap and read to the three girls. Kyle and Ben played in the barn after chasing the cat up a tree and trying unsuccessfully to coax it down again. Tess and Fran, worn out from the morning, fell asleep on the sofa.

"Mom, is their dad going to be okay?" Jane was helping Liz in the kitchen, putting away the last of the dishes from their meal.

"I hope so, honey. Should we pray for him and his family?" Jane nodded solemnly and listened as her mom spoke simple words asking for healing for Kent.

When the phone rang Liz caught it on the second ring. "Liz. This is Jay." A pause. "He's going to make it." She exhaled. "We're in Kearney at the regional hospital. The Life Flight air ambulance came and got him after the hospital in Benton stabilized him. How's everyone doing there?"

"Everyone's fine. How's Bonnie?"

"She's doing okay. Pretty worried. The doctors keep updating us."

"What happened?" Liz's face told Jane what their half of the conversation hadn't revealed. Fran's dad was going to be okay.

"A truck tipped, pinning him underneath. He was up early, trying to get yesterday's harvested corn unloaded, when one of his truckers drove by him. They were working on the side of a hill and the grain must have shifted. The truck went over. It's going to be some time before he's back in the saddle but he's going to make it."

She struggled to keep her voice even. "I am so glad you called. The kids have been very worried. I've been worried," she added with feeling.

"Liz, I need to ask a favor. Bonnie wants me to take the kids to church in the morning. Wants them to feel like everything's going to be fine and to do what they'd normally do. Would you mind helping them find some clothes at the ranch?"

"Of course. What time's church?"

"It's early this week. Our priest alternates Mass times with the Catholic church in Pearse, at 8:30 and 10:30. See you about quarter after eight. And Liz?"

"Yes?"

"Thanks." She held the phone a few seconds after he hung up.

That's what she'd meant about Mike, she thought. A family who would be there for one another, especially when everything wasn't smooth. She returned the phone to its base and looked at her daughter.

"Go find the older boys, honey. We're going over to the Robbins place to get some clothes. They're going to stay with us tonight. Won't that be fun?"

She gently woke Tess and Fran. Patrick came out of the downstairs bedroom, rubbing his eyes and yawning. It was a squeeze but the kids seemed good natured about the ride in Liz's car.

She supervised piles of clothes and toothbrushes. After they'd loaded the trunk, Sugar came up to Liz, wagging her tail in anticipation. "All right," she said reluctantly, "jump in the back seat. And don't lick," she warned the dog.

They broiled hamburgers and made a fruit salad for supper. A fair amount of lemonade was spilled on the counter and dribbled down to the floor, but at least the kids were pitching in to help.

Bedtime came after baths and showers. The boys shared Ben's room and Fran joined Tess and Jane in their room. Kyle swore that Sugar slept in their parents' room and Sugar pressed for the same consideration.

"She's lucky to get past the porch," Liz told Kyle. "Sugar can sleep in the living room but that's as far as she gets." She mothered each child with a hug and a warning to get to sleep quickly since church was early. Several groans accompanied the word church.

Walking wearily down the steps, she surveyed the downstairs and began picking up, quickly scrubbing the sticky spots in the kitchen and making preparations for morning. In bed by ten, Liz tumbled into a deep, untroubled sleep, where she dreamt of a car full of kids, a cat with a sloppy grin, and a windshield wiper resembling a wagging tail.

She rose early. Emerging from her room in the dark of the morning, she stumbled over Sugar and landed hard on her big square coffee table. Liz screamed at the pain in her side. Her arm only slightly broke her fall. Sugar, yelping and flailing to regain her footing, came back to lick Liz in apology. "Leave me alone." More licks. "I'm all right, ok?" She pushed the dog away.

She lay there for some time, trying to even out her breathing. When she could fill her lungs without crying out, she struggled to her feet and led the dog through the dark, silent house to the porch.

Walking by the kitchen and now reminded of her morning chores, she showered and made breakfast. It was a kid's breakfast; juice, sausage, blueberry muffins, and the cold cereals she and her kids could agree on.

Ben and Jane came downstairs about the time she finished, so she sent them off to wake the rest of the household. The six were to dress and come to the table.

Jay drove the Robbins Suburban in at 8:20, his face shadowed with a day's growth of stubble. "I left my pickup for Bonnie," he told Liz. "I thought this would fit the four of us a little better."

"Eight. We're coming, too." If he was surprised, he didn't show it, but instead he stepped into the living room. The Daniels and Robbins kids were sitting on the floor listening as Kyle read aloud from his newest adventure book.

Jay looked back at Liz, dressed in a rust colored pant suit, her hair gleaming, make-up applied softly, and shook his head in wonder. "You're something. Suddenly a mother of six and look at you."

"I didn't spend the night in a hospital waiting room," she countered gently. "By comparison, this is easy." She lowered her voice. "How is your brother?"

"He's doing pretty well, considering. He's got a hell of a long way to go. The doctors say he will need a lot of rehab." He shook his head. "Bonnie's a real trooper, too. She's keeping her head and that's keeping him steady."

He stepped closer, brushing her cheek with his finger tips. "Thanks for everything you're doing for my family." Then he looked at his watch and called into the next room. "Hey! Anyone coming?"

The kids clamored to his side, full of halting questions. They moved out to the Suburban and quickly loaded up for the short drive, Jay answering their questions as best he could.

Parking half a block from the old church, he took Patrick by the hand and led the way into a pew near the middle on the right side. All of the kids entered the pew and knelt, Daniels kids included. Jay glanced at Liz, who brought up the rear. She too knelt.

It felt good to be back, Liz decided. Leaving Minneapolis was her time to leave everything she knew. Now it was time to take back everything that meant something to her.

At Communion time she stood back, making room for the kids to go up to the front of the church first. Jay paused, waiting for her to go ahead of him.

The church goers watched Jay and Liz and their families in silent approval. In the face of the Robbins family troubles, they collectively decided, some good might just come out of this tragedy.

Several people stood outside after church. Jay introduced Liz to Father Bob Monroe who welcomed her family to St. Mary's parish, then encouraged her to send her children to religious education classes. She agreed to bring them the following Wednesday evening.

Jay, surrounded by questions about his older brother, answered calmly. "I don't know how long." "Yes, he was lucky." "I'm not sure." "He was looking a little better this morning." "No, no one else was hurt." and "I hope so."

As people drifted off to their vehicles he turned to Liz. "What's this about you sending your kids to Wednesday night classes?"

She simply smiled. "We'd better get going, Jay. We've got a full day ahead." She gathered her charges and walked to the Suburban.

An old classmate, overhearing, and having been similarly summoned, issued Jay a good natured warning. "Watch out, buddy. If you're not careful that could well be the beginning of a long line of such orders."

Jay's comeback, "Wouldn't bother me. I could get used to this," was repeated that week in more than a few conversations.

Debra touched Jay's jacket sleeve and told him to ignore her husband. "John's just jealous because he's remembering when we first dated. He's dreaming of a return to those magical days, right, hon?" Her comment sent both men to their cars.

Jay drove to the Mustang Café and picked up the Sunday Kearney paper. Tossing it onto Liz's lap as he got back in the Suburban, he asked what she had in mind for the day.

"Just head us out home and you'll see." He squinted his eyes, surprised again by this woman.

"You know," he told Liz after the boys had climbed over the girls to get to the house first, "when we first met I liked you right away. But darlin', you're making it difficult for me to behave myself these days."

Liz, ignoring his words, got out and carried the newspaper toward the house. Jay was around the side of the Suburban before she saw him, swinging her into his arms.

The last of the girls, just emerging from the Suburban, squealed as Jay carried Liz up the porch steps and into the kitchen, setting her down on the counter, his devilish grin a few inches from her flustered face. Newspaper sections rained to the floor around them.

She was dealing with a man who was letting it be known he wanted her and she couldn't, for the life of her, think, let alone breathe. She uttered the first thought she could raise. "Jay, the kids, they're…"

"Going upstairs," he finished for her. "Hey! You're the one who's flirting with me, tilting me off balance." Mass trampling up the stairs could be heard as the kids raced to change out of church clothes. "I doubt if it's new to Kent's kids to see the adults mess around a little. And if it's new to your kids, God help them."

His hands about her waist, he waited. For all his obvious pursuit, it was her call. He'd promised time and space and he was going to keep that promise.

Flushed, Liz returned his look. "No, Mike and I never goofed around like this," she finally whispered. "In front of the kids or otherwise. I wish we could have." Her eyes dropped to his lips.

Suddenly Tess was at Jay's feet, "Mom? Can you untie my dress? Jane says I should be able to reach clear back behind me and I can't and she won't listen. She just wants to play with Fran and leave me out."

Her eyes locked on his, Liz gently pushed Jay back and slid to the floor. "Jane should have helped, shouldn't she? There you go, it's untied. Make sure you hang it up!" she called after Tess as her baby girl ran off, fair hair flying behind her.

"Suppose you could make yourself useful around here?" Liz asked as she moved around to the other side of the table.

"Oh yeah, I could," Jay chuckled, stepping toward her.

"I mean," she was speaking a little too quickly but couldn't help it, "could you help me get some food ready?"

"I was just kidding," although the look on his face said otherwise. "What do you want done?"

"I need," she emphasized, drawing a raised brow, "you to make a bunch of sandwiches while I pack some chips and fruit. There's some sliced meat in the fridge and the bread's over there." She pointed to the corner of the counter near the sink windows.

She could feel her pulse slowing now that there was some space between them. "I thought we could make a picnic lunch and eat it in Kearney and then go to the hospital. I've noticed a neat little park by the shopping center when I've been there. That way Bonnie could see her kids. I think she'd like that."

"That sounds good," Jay said, reaching for the loaf of bread. Liz handed him her cutting board and a knife. "It's hard on Bonnie to be pulled two ways but she's where she needs to be. Probably for some time." His light mood didn't quite mask his worry.

She saw this. "Jay." He looked up. "He's going to be okay. I just know it. Feel it. In church this morning, I felt a powerful warmth wrap around me."

"Those were my good wishes sent your way, darlin'."

She looked away. "I'm serious."

"I know," he said, and leaned back against the counter. "I guess I just feel useless right now with Kent and Bon. Then I get back here and you're doing great with all the kids. After what you've been through and trying to do all of this yourself. I'm not just falling for you, Liz. I'm there."

"Jay, don't. It's too ... I don't want this." Her hands gripped a package of paper plates to her chest.

"Shhh," he said, putting his finger up to her lips and brushing her hair back to the side of her face. "Here it is. I'm falling in love with you."

He'd come around the side of the table and was now standing in front of her. "I'm telling you right now so that whatever happens from here on between you and me you won't think it's just some kind of grateful reaction on my part. You decide how you feel and what comes next. I'll give you that because you deserve it. I'm going to pursue you because I like you and I want to be with you. Just let me see you sometimes, will you?"

His goofy, hang dog look was her undoing. Laughter rushed from her constricted throat even as tears streamed down her face. He stood watching her, letting her cry it out.

She grabbed a paper napkin from the counter and wiped her eyes, then blew her nose. "I don't feel very much in control." She blew again. "After Bonnie drove off I kept thinking about what she was feeling. I couldn't have handled it."

"Yeah, you could have," Jay assured her. He handed her another napkin, bending down to look into her eyes, giving her a heads-up nod. "It's not easy having all these kids dependent on you and yet you're doing it. And they're doing fine because of you."

He straightened up. "Hang in there." Jay turned his attention to his sandwich job.

They put the food in a large cooler and took along an insulated container of lemonade, loading all of it in the back of the Suburban. Liz had noticed bruises starting on her side when she'd changed into jeans and a sweater, so she'd taken a few aspirin and shrugged off the pain and stiffness. Ben was sent back to the house to change into more presentable jeans and then they left.

They found a place in the park to eat where it was sunny yet out of the wind. Kyle had brought along a football and he and Ben chose teams after they'd eaten. Although the game may well end in arguments or tears, for now all six were deep into the competition.

Liz lounged on the blanket, lazily watching them play. Jay had picked up the trash and found a Dumpster while she'd assembled the leftovers. He came back and had no more then squatted down to say something when Kyle and Patrick came running up to him, begging his help as a referee. It turned out not everyone agreed on the rules, let alone which down it was.

"I'll be there in a minute," Jay assured them. They walked away, certain in their youthful knowledge that it would be more like ten. "Did you hear the news? Roger asked Annie to marry him Friday night."

Liz bolted upright. Annie had left a message on Liz's answering machine yesterday morning to see how her date had gone the night before and to please call her, that she had something to tell her. But she'd been outside with the kids and later, after Bonnie, had completely forgotten to call her back.

"Roger called me first thing yesterday morning and asked me to be his best man. They're talking about sometime over Christmas break so they can have some honeymoon time.

Annie, thought Liz. Annie's getting married.

Jay reached for the blanket and playfully tugged on it. "We'd better get going. Maybe you and Annie can have some time together after we get everybody back home and I can try to figure out the week ahead."

"Sounds good," Liz said, getting up.

He picked up the blanket and shook off the leaves and grass.

Liz touched his arm. "I don't know anything about harvesting or cattle, Jay. But kids I do know. They can stay with me unless Bonnie has another idea."

He shook his head. "There are plenty of other people in the neighborhood and in town who can help out, Liz. My sister and her husband were gone this weekend to the Nebraska football game and we haven't been able to reach them yet but when they get back she'll want to help with the kids, too. You've got plenty going on already."

Liz persisted. "Just see what Bonnie says. If she's okay with it, I can handle the details."

Jay let it rest. It wasn't Liz's problem to watch his niece and nephews. He was sure Bonnie would see it the same way. He handed Liz the blanket and jogged over to where the football game had become a muddle.

Liz thought back to before Mike. She'd been happy, working hard, in love with life. She had liked where she was living, how she spent her free time, and had little chaos in her life.

It feels that way now, she realized. There were terrible challenges in the Robbins family with the accident, their farm commodity prices, the long hours and the poor financial returns they faced, and still there was so much love and support.

Liz remembered her first impression of Benton after she had settled in. Home. It had felt like her home in such a short time. If I keep heading in this direction, she thought, surely it will get easier each day to feel comfortable, to eventually have the constant uneasiness in my life go away.

Footsteps crunching dry leaves brought Liz back to the park. Jay stood in front of her, reaching for the food containers. She handed them over and walked with him to the parking lot.

Bonnie's response was not the one Jay had expected. The kids could stay with Liz for now. After a brief stop in Kent's room, Jay brought Bonnie out to the waiting area.

Patrick, Fran, and Kyle reached for their mother, and more than a few tears were shed. After a while, they quieted. "Your dad's going to get good help here, and be back home with us as soon as he can," Bonnie promised.

Jay took Bonnie aside to discuss the doctor's comments from the morning rounds. Finally he called Liz over to join them. "Bonnie said that will be fine, you're having the kids there with you." His voice held a combination of gratitude and reluctance.

The two women hugged, their eyes locked in heart talk. "I'll feel easier knowing the kids are close to home. Thank you for offering, Liz." No demonstrations. Bonnie would need to let others help.

"Jay, I think Kent wants to talk to you again before you go."

"I'll go in right now. Anything else you need?"

"No, that's all I can think of for now." She kissed his cheek.

The women watched him return to intensive care. "He's been a friend of mine forever," Bonnie said, looking at Liz. "We even dated back in high school. After Kent, I don't think there's anyone I'd trust more than him."

Liz returned Bonnie's look, then asked if she needed some clothes gathered and sent to her.

Bonnie was exhausted but she gave Liz a thin smile. "That would be great. And some make-up and such. All of it's in the bathroom next to our bedroom. Fran can show you. Our suitcases are in the basement near the laundry room."

"Oh, and Liz..." Bonnie had started back to her husband's room, then remembered something. "I meant what I said about Jay."

Liz was amazed at Bonnie's strength. "I believe you. My ex-husband was not like Jay. I wish I'd..." But Jay came up the hallway and Liz broke off the rest. Bonnie squeezed her hand and walked back to the intensive care unit.

His conversation with Kent on his mind, Jay hurried everyone back down to the main lobby. "I'm going to take my truck home. You go ahead and drive the kids, if you would, Liz. Bonnie doesn't need a vehicle right now and she wants you to have enough room."

He handed her the keys. "I'd better get going," he said, brushing her hair behind her ear. Jay walked to the far end of the parking lot and started his pickup. Her response to him this time didn't scare her. And that shook her.

Halfway to the Suburban, Liz decided to call Annie. Before they could leave the lobby a second time, some of the kids needed to stop in the restrooms, so it was after 3:30 before they drove out of town.

On the way home, Liz had time for some long overdue reflection. She hadn't burnt any bridges at The Source, the Minneapolis PR firm where she had worked. They had even hinted at sending some work to her at the time she was leaving.

Whether they were simply being polite or not, they'd extended the offer. She decided to follow up and see if she could get some contract work.

By installing a couple extra phone lines and hooking up local Internet access, Liz could be in business. She could be home when the kids were home and really push when they were at school. If it was working for Roger, it could work for her.

The miles sped by as she made plans, and she soon arrived at the Robbins ranch. An hour later they'd gathered clothes, toys, school books, sleeping bags, a trumpet, and Bonnie's items, and were back at the Red Door, rearranging bedrooms to accommodate everyone as much as possible.

Sugar's barks and wagging tail alerted Liz to Annie's arrival. She'd brought more than pizza and soda. Some kind of outdoor adventure movie was popped into the VCR and quiet descended for the first time in hours.

Bunched around the coffee table with their paper plates and cups, the six kids became immersed in the film.

"First," Liz said to Annie as they walked into the kitchen, "thanks for the feast. You saved me tonight. Second," she hugged Annie, "I can't believe my best friend is engaged and I wasn't here to talk."

Liz choked up, then laughed self-consciously. Annie grinned at her and wiped her eyes.

"Third," Liz said, "Jay told me the wedding is at Christmas time. That's only eight weeks away. I don't think I'll be ready to lose you that soon."

Annie was beaming. "Your life will be even more interesting by then, me thinks."

Liz stared at Annie. "I have no idea what you're talking about." She picked up a slice of pizza and took a bite.

"Oh? Roger tells me Jay is walking a few inches off the ground. Hasn't said a word, mind you, but from what I hear, your Jay is smitten. Hard."

Liz took her time swallowing.

Annie was eyeing her, head tilted in her *you can tell me* manner. "Well?"

"Annie, for one thing, no one uses the word smitten anymore. No one. It's probably not even in the dictionary anymore. Don't be ridiculous. I barely know him."

She took another bite and sat forward, thoughtfully munching. "Remember not all that long ago when I was on your sun porch talking about my marriage break up? And I told you about the computer solitaire I'd been playing? You thought I was nuts. Yeah, you did," Liz insisted to Annie's quick denial.

She rushed on before she could be interrupted. "I still find it fascinating how each slightly different move can make such a radical change in the big picture. There's so much about life that's just a flip of the card, and Annie, I'm scared of the odds." Getting up she walked to the counter and offered Annie a slice, then peeked in on the group in the living room.

"That's it? That's all you're going to tell me? Liz, Roger tells me more than that and he's a guy." Annie sat with her hands on her hips, her lips parted.

"That's all I've got to say for now," Liz answered firmly. They talked about Annie and Roger's plans and about Kent's accident and prognosis. After the movie, the kids did their homework and were sent to bed.

Annie noticed Liz's stiff, slow movements, and heard about Sugar's Statue of Liberty tackle early that morning. They agreed to meet Friday at the homecoming game, and then Annie headed home.

Liz prepared for a rushed morning breakfast with six kids and a 7:45 bus. She slept well a second night in a row.

6

Ruby Morrison noticed Jay walking up the Dirt Store's sidewalk. He'd bought several shrubs for his grandparents' place this year but Ruby had a feeling that it wasn't business he had on his mind today. Liz's hurried call that morning had her concerned. Maybe Jay knew something.

"Morning, Ruby. Can I talk to Liz?"

"Good morning, Jay. She's not working this morning. Called in and asked for some personal time off. Said she'd be back in time to help out before the noon hour."

"Any idea where she went?"

"Sorry," Ruby shook her head. "She didn't say." And he knew Ruby wouldn't intrude.

Asking her to mention he'd been there, he left and drove over to Benton Public School. Annie was directing traffic during a change in classes.

"What brings you back to these hallowed halls? Needing a brush up?" she teased.

He grinned in response.

Then more seriously, "I was sorry to hear about Kent, Jay. Liz says he's going to be all right. I'm so glad."

"Thanks, Annie. I hear congratulations are in order. I wish all the best to you and Rog. Speaking of Liz, any idea where she is? I checked at the Dirt Store but she took the morning off."

"She didn't mention anything last night." She glanced at her room clock and then called down the hallway. "Tom, Lora, get a move on." She waved the loitering students into her classroom. "Knowledge doesn't wait. I wonder, Jay, if you might find her at the clinic. I'd better get back to work. Good seeing you."

He parked in front of the clinic next to Liz's car and walked up to the receptionist's desk where Mary Sue Parker was talking on the phone. "Gotta go, Marge. Jay Robbins is here to see me. Bye."

She smiled a very warm welcome. Mary Sue had always been surrounded by males in high school, he remembered, even if she had walked into their midst and not the other way around.

"Well, Jay, I must say this is an unexpected pleasure. What can I do for you today?"

"Mary Sue, it's good to see you, too. I'm looking for Liz Daniels. Is she here?"

"Liz Daniels. Do I know her?"

Jay realized this could take some time. "I don't know if you two have had the pleasure, Mary Sue, but I believe that's her car out front. I just need a few minutes to visit with her."

"Oh, yes, now I know to whom you're referring. She's not here. She left quite a while ago."

And then she was absorbed in sorting through message slips on her desk. If it was no longer interesting to Mary Sue, it simply wasn't important.

He caught Ida Martin's eye behind a stack of files. She'd worked in medical records since the clinic had been built. Ida motioned toward the back door leading from the clinic to the hospital across the alley. He nodded his thanks and went out the door.

Jay walked through the emergency door and to the nurse's station where a pair of tennis shoes dangled from the counter top. Patrick's shoes. The boy was giggling and making faces for his newfound friends. Uncle and nephew greeted one another and Jay lifted Patrick down from the counter.

By now more than a little confused, Jay asked the first nurse.

"She's down the hall in treatment room two. She'll be out in..."

He had Patrick's hand in his and they were walking down the hall before she could get the rest out. Patty had known Jay since second grade. "Wouldn't have done any good to tell him to wait," she said to the younger nurse seated beside her. "Jay's a Robbins and that must rhyme with 'bull headed' in some language."

The Physician's assistant had just left the room. Behind the door was a voice, Liz's voice, saying thank you. Jay knocked and heard a soft "Come in." He opened the door and caught sight of a brace wrapped around her mid-section as she struggled to pull on her sweatshirt.

Looking up, Liz's eyes flashed. Patrick followed Jay in the room and pulled on her arm, asking if they could now go to the park. Liz winced and stifled a low moan.

"Just a minute, Pat," Jay said. "We'll go soon."

Noticing a wooden puzzle on a shelf, he lifted the boy up onto the other end of the examining table and set him to work. Then Jay took Liz's second sleeve and carefully, slowly eased her arm through. "What happened?" he asked.

"You know, this is supposed to be a private place and I should be able to come here in...in privacy," she finished shortly.

She was angry — angry at the pain, at herself for letting the stupid dog in the house, at Jay for finding her like this.

Slowly easing down off the table, Liz reached for her purse. A sharp pain in her side brought her up short of air and groaning once more.

Jay picked up her purse and, lifting Patrick down from his perch, opened the door. Liz stalked past, mad at the world.

They emerged into a stormy Monday morning. Dark gray clouds had been building to the south all morning and now the wind was picking up. Some paper trash was bouncing down the main street and two young boys on bikes were rushing to get somewhere. Matches my mood perfectly, Liz decided. And to prove it she slammed her car door after her.

"So what's next on your agenda?" Jay asked, leaning on her door. He was close enough so that she could see his concern. It was a good thing, too, or she'd probably explode.

He tried again. "Patrick and I are headed to the east park. I kind of hoped we could meet there and swing awhile." He handed her purse through the window and seeing her glower, didn't wait for a reply.

Jay gave her a few minutes before arriving. He came to sit next to her on the swings, as Patrick ran to the tornado slide. "I wasn't trying to tick you off," he explained. "I was worried when no one knew where you and Pat had gone. And I guess I just couldn't resist seeing what kind of temper you've got."

After trying out the swing, he added, "It's like mine; infrequent but noticeable."

She sighed heavily. A little friend had joined Patrick and was making the sliding a lot more fun. "I suppose it was my car parked out front of the clinic. I can't get used to everyone knowing my business."

"No, it was my network of spies," he joked. "I stopped at the store this morning looking for you, and you were already gone when I headed back into town from checking on things at Kent's. Ruby didn't know where you were so I talked to Annie at school and she thought maybe the clinic. Tell me, how did you get past Mary Sue?"

She fluttered her eyelashes. "Why I just let her win the first round. After that I wasn't any fun."

He laughed, testing the swing once again and asked how long she'd known Mary Sue.

"We just met," she admitted.

"You're fast."

"Apparently not fast enough." She carefully tried out her swing. "I tripped over Sugar and bruised two ribs and hurt my arm."

He touched her knee, sorry for her pain. "This morning?

"No. Yesterday, early, before breakfast and church. It was okay during the day but last night I was having trouble breathing deeply and this morning I was challenged getting out of bed."

They turned when they heard Patrick and his friend yelling as they raced for the double slide.

She noticed lines on Jay's face and thought to ask about Kent. She knew he would have called his sister-in-law first thing in the morning.

"He sounds better," he answered, relief in his voice. "Bonnie said he had a good night. They're hoping to move him out of intensive care in a couple days. He has to pass a few more tests and then they'll slowly start into rehab."

Jay tugged lightly on her swing's chain. "I'm not prying into your business, Liz. I was just worried when you and Pat were missing. And I'm sorry about your ribs and arm. You're probably wondering, along with Darlene, what the hell you're doing here."

"You will never know me well enough to believe that I think that is funny." But she chuckled when she said it, then gasped.

"What are you going to do now?" he asked, watching her manage the pain.

"I think," she answered reluctantly, "I'm going to have to go home for a while and rest. I didn't get much sleep last night. The PA gave me some pain pills to help me get through the next few days."

Jay offered to take Patrick off her hands. He was meeting with some neighbors to organize the remainder of Kent's harvest. In the afternoon he would start looking for some hands to help him wean. Cattle work would follow quickly on the heels of the grain harvest, and finding help, particularly good help, would again be tough.

Even though Jay had been helping his brother on an occasional basis, additional labor was needed for the big fall jobs. If he started looking today, Jay told Liz, hopefully he would have people on board by the time they were needed.

Despite his own house project and the job in Kearney to which he should be attending, Jay knew he'd be in the saddle gathering cattle from pastures, sorting calves, and loading trailers some time over the next couple weeks.

Liz listened intently as he talked. Accepting a hand up, she walked over to her car, stopping to tell Patrick he was to go with Jay.

They'd be back in time for supper, Jay assured her as she started her car, and he'd like to stay and help if she didn't mind. Moving in tandem and working out details, much of their former uneasiness seemed to be leaving.

"You are welcome," she said. "You don't need to bring anything or do anything. I think you could probably use an evening off." She drove off to bed.

Jay called over to his nephew. "Ready to go, Pat? Want something to drink?" That brought him on a run. When Jay opened his door, the little boy jumped up on the running board and climbed over to the passenger side.

"She's something, isn't she?" Jay said, forgetting who was with him.

"Who? " Patrick piped up, "Aunt Liz?"

"Is that what you call her?" Jay looked at him curiously.

"Yup," he said as he bobbed his head seriously. "I like her."

Jay's lips curved. "Me too. How 'bout some soda at the café?"

೫೦೦೩

The sound of her phone awakened Liz from a crazy, jumbled dream. It was a mix of people and places swirling in and out of focus, nothing making sense.

She'd thought to bring the phone in by the bed, so she was able to answer after only a few rings. "Hello?"

"Liz, how are you? It's Kevin."

She struggled to sit up, willing her voice to stay even. "Kevin. It's good to hear from you. How's everyone at The Source?"

"Hey, business is good. Very good. Actually, that's why I'm calling. How would you like to come back to work? I've talked it over with Pete and Sandra. We could ship you a computer, printer, fax, the works."

Liz winced at another sliver of pain. "Why? What's up?"

Kevin pitched. "We're running behind all the time and it sure would beat having to hire someone new. We'd send you contract work. You'd give us the same good things you always gave us. What do you think? You game? Exactly what are you doing in Nebraska anyway?"

He wouldn't believe her if she told him. "I was just thinking of calling you. And I just might take you up on your proposition. What kind of money are we talking here?"

"Tell you what," his voice faded as he briefly turned his head away from the phone, "I've got to get to an appointment right now. Let me know what you decide. Gotta go." The line went dead.

She clicked off, then on again, and phoned directory assistance for the Kearney airport. After making arrangements, she called Ruby and told her she would again need some time off.

"Don't you worry, Liz. We'll do fine here. It's slowing down now."

Then she had Annie paged at school. "Absolutely. I'd be glad to watch your kids. You really bruised two ribs? Wow, what a dog."

By the time the kids arrived home on the bus, Liz had called back to Minneapolis, was packed, and had snacks and a supper lined up. She was ready to go when Annie arrived.

Waving out of her car window, she drove to Kearney, pushing the speed limit the whole way. After making the connection in Omaha, Liz settled back and slept all the way to the Twin Cities.

As soon as she checked into her motel room, she took another pain pill and ordered room service.

That evening, Jay and Patrick arrived for supper and were met by Annie and crew. Ben, having felt Jay's absence, was especially pleased to see him, and jostled for a close position.

By the time Annie sent the kids to wash up for supper, Jay's patience was stretched to breaking point.

"He was really ticked," Annie told Liz later on the phone. "I think he arrived all prepared to take care of you and here he is, with all these kids, and me, and you've vanished again. Between being worn out and worried about his brother, he'd had it. I really felt bad for him."

"What did you say?" Liz asked.

"I told him all I know is that you called me and asked if I could come out after I got off work and stay with the kids tonight. That you said you would be back tomorrow afternoon before they got off the bus and you were flying to Minneapolis on some business. Something about a job. He was pretty mad. Then when I said the word 'job' he got real quiet."

"I'm sorry you had to go through that," Liz said, "being the messenger, I mean."

"So what's the plan?" Annie asked, walking to Liz's porch to let Sugar back inside.

"I meet with The Source people tomorrow morning, seven-thirty, and push for the best deal I can get. They know my work and I know the job, so this is a terrific opportunity for me. It means I can earn some good money doing what I like doing and the kids and I can take care of ourselves."

⊱⊰

By three the next afternoon, Jay was south of agitated. He'd decided to work on the house to keep his mind off Liz, but it hadn't worked. Worried about her and her injuries, he was afraid he was going to lose her before he'd ever had her.

Kent noticed his bad mood immediately. Jay had walked into his brother's room early that morning, bringing along the bag Liz had gathered for Bonnie. They had been talking about ranch work that needed to be done.

"What's eating you, little brother?" Jay jerked his head around, having forgotten where he was. Kent was eyeing him, an amused expression lighting up his wan face.

"Nothing. About the calves; once we've got them sorted off, where do you want them put?" They discussed how to go about weaning this year's calf crop.

Jay helped his brother take a drink of water from a straw. Again his mind drifted.

"Why don't you just spit it out," Kent said pointedly.

Jay frowned. He started to deny there was anything on his mind, then decided otherwise. "I feel like a damn fool. Like a young kid with his first girlfriend."

Kent stayed quiet.

Jay began pacing, hands shoved deep in his jeans pockets. "Did you ever wonder, after you

and Bonnie were...had some kind of understanding, if she felt like you did? If your feelings
were the same?"

"No, I never questioned her feelings," Kent
said. "But I remember a few times then and a few
thousand times since when I noticed we weren't
on the same wavelength." Jay returned to his
chair by the bed.

Kent gained steam as he realized this
marked the first time his brother had asked him
for this kind of advice. "You know enough about
women, or people in general, to know you never
really know them, understand them. But with
that special person it's a real battle because we
want to and it's not possible. You and I don't understand each other that perfectly either, but we
don't care. Don't care to, either!" He chuckled
softly.

Jay slumped back in his chair, resigned to
his brother's enjoyment of the moment.

"What's going on?"

"Liz left for Minneapolis a couple hours after I saw her yesterday and didn't say a damn
word about her trip to me. And that was after we
made plans to eat supper at her place. Annie
watched the kids last night and said Liz was going to some job interview and would be back this
afternoon. To be honest," he looked away, "I'm
scared Benton and I aren't enough to hold her."

"Would you go to Minneapolis for her?" Kent
asked quietly.

Jay scowled. "What the hell kind of a stupid
question is that?" he said with heat.

Kent drove home his point. "Women are asked to drop everything, move into our lives, and in many cases adapt to a totally foreign environment out here. Would you do that for her, move into hers?"

Jay thought for a while and answered quietly. "Yes, in a minute. And I don't know. Both. I hope it doesn't come to that."

Now, as Jay was banging hammer on nail and walking aimlessly around the house doing a little job here, picking up something there, the day was dragging. Finally he called the airport and asked when her flight would arrive. It had landed two hours earlier but they couldn't guarantee who had been on it.

Fifteen minutes later, Liz's car stopped in front of his house. He saw her slide out of the seat and, shading her eyes, look up at the house.

She shut the car door and slowly walked up the sidewalk, pushing the doorbell twice. Uncertain whether it was yet wired, she swung the door open and called out. "Jay? It's Liz. Are you here?"

She was waiting for him, standing near the bottom of the winding staircase. He stepped down off of the last step and touched her arm. "How are you doing? How are the ribs?"

"I'm fine. Tired. We need to talk." A few minutes later they were sitting at a booth in the back of the Mustang. "I stopped at the hospital. Your brother was looking better; he thought he might be starting therapy next week." Jay nodded but said nothing.

She twisted her napkin. "Anyway," she cleared her throat, "he said you'd been down this morning. Then Kent said something kind of odd, something about you being in worse shape than your sophomore year when you broke your leg at the end of football two-a-days."

She thought for a moment. "I'm sorry I didn't reach you to cancel dinner last night." In a quieter voice, she added, "This is really hard for me."

He jumped on that. "What's hard for you? I thought we'd made plans."

They were interrupted by the arrival of their coffee. Liz thanked Connie who took her time in leaving their booth. Jay had already caused a stir when he'd first returned home, eyed by single women and a few married ones. But now something was going on between him and the woman from Minnesota, and quite a few people wanted to know what.

Liz brushed aside his anger, determined to answer his question politely. "I just kind of mentally clicked off what I had to get done and I got Annie to watch the kids for me. I was in a hurry and I'm afraid I didn't think about you, how you would feel. I wasn't functioning very well, I guess."

She reached for her coffee, had it halfway to her mouth when she saw the glitter in his eyes. She held up her hand, determined to keep a handle on her temper. "Jay, it's a job opportunity with my former employer." Still no response. "You're doing your work. What possible business is it of yours what I do?" She needed her pain pills.

"I would have thought you could have mentioned your trip," he said through tight lips. "I feel like a fool, thought we were coming to an understanding. I enjoyed this weekend with you despite all the..." he searched briefly for a civilized word, then gave up the attempt, "damned shit that went with it. And now you tell me you're heading back to the big city, for a job?"

Liz opened her mouth to respond when she saw Roger walk in, notice the two of them, and head toward their booth. "I'd be happy to talk with you about this if you would stop with the possessive thing," she said in a low tone.

Then, seeing Arch and Patrick enter the café a few steps behind Roger, she rushed to finish. "But I sincerely doubt it would do any good. You're right. I'm wrong. Do I have that down correctly?" She lifted her eyebrows, daring him to argue.

Liz stood as Roger approached the table and greeted him. Turning back to Jay, she said goodbye. "The kids will be getting off the bus in a few minutes and I need to be there." She spoke a few words to Arch and left the café, Patrick in tow.

Roger and Arch joined Jay, tactfully ignoring the thunderous look on his face. Labeling himself a certifiable fool, Jay knew Liz had seen Benton and been back to Minneapolis. Benton had lost.

Liz had no desire to see Jay that night, not that he stopped. She spent the rest of the week quietly going about her work. By Friday night, she was feeling the effects of their argument, incomplete as it had been.

"I keep telling myself that work and my kids, you, my new friends here—this is what I want. This is enough. I just didn't realize he had moved into my life that much."

"I thought you didn't want a man within fifty feet," Annie observed coolly. They were standing in the school parking lot as people streamed around them and onto the edges of the football field. "You ought to feel relieved he's gone."

The whole area was lit by the bright glow from stadium lights set atop old windmill towers. Liz's kids ran off to join their friends. A rowdy football game was being organized on the sidelines by little boys anxious to be old enough to play on the real field.

It was a big game with a big rival. The high school conference championship likely would hinge on who won tonight. Kent and Jay's sister had driven up that afternoon from Kearney to take the Robbins kids for the weekend. At the moment, Liz was feeling light.

"Well, I am," Liz said softly, slowly, her conviction lacking.

Annie pushed a little harder. "Didn't you want it simple? Dig dirt and no relationships?"

"No impossible relationships," Liz countered, confused by her own apparent defense of Jay.

Annie smiled into the darkness. "If you say so. Say, that reminds me," she said, nodding her head toward the school. "There's something I want to show you. Follow me."

Entering a side door with her keys and turning on her room lights, Annie walked over to several piles of faded papers and sifted through them, searching for something. Liz remained in the doorway.

"Now where did I put it?" she murmured, taking off her red wool poncho and tossing it on a chair so she could dig more easily. After a few minutes, she held up a paper. "Here it is. I knew it was in this stack." Annie triumphantly waved it at Liz and handed it to her on their way out.

"What's this?"

Annie clicked off the lights and locked her classroom door. "Just a little something I came across in a box stuffed in the back of my storage closet. Something you said just now reminded me of it," Annie said. She led the way down the hall and out the back door.

She pulled her poncho on over her head and looked around, searching for someone. "I'll see you in the stands. I promised Jan I'd fill in for her at the ticket booth so she could go eat. She's probably wondering where I am."

Liz climbed halfway up the bleachers and found a space for Annie and herself to sit. The game got off to a strong start with the Benton Mustangs making several big plays. Both teams hit hard.

She noticed an intermingling of the communities. People were visiting with one another up and down both sides of the field. Glancing at the paper on her lap, Liz was shocked to read the name typed across the bottom of the first page: JAY M. ROBBINS.

"Good game, isn't it?" Annie asked as she squeezed in next to her. Looks like we've got us a real contest. Here, want some popcorn?" She offered to share.

Liz folded the papers and stuffed them into her stadium jacket pocket. They munched on popcorn and followed the battle unfolding before them, laughing at the antics of some of the more serious fans in the crowd and yelling with everyone else when Benton scored at the end of the half to catch up with the opposing team.

They were taking a stretch, standing near the concession stand, when a distinctive voice wafted over. "I suppose she's interesting because she's not from here. I mean, some guys are attracted for a while to that foreign element." It was Mary Sue Parker, and she had an audience waiting in line to buy sodas, chili dogs, and nachos.

"She really isn't Jay's type," the voice droned on. "I've seen a few of his women friends and not one of them had little kids dangling from their arms. If it lasts as long as his other flings lasted, we'll see one of us on his arm pretty soon."

Annie nudged her friend. "You aren't going to pay attention to that. There's a Mary Sue Parker or two in every community."

"I know," Liz said wearily, "but I'd love to set her straight. My kids do not dangle."

Annie grinned. "Ah, forget her. Here come the boys onto the field again. Let's head back up where we can see better." Liz walked a few steps and stopped abruptly.

Annie walked in close and in a low voice muttered, "Nothing anyone says means anything. The only thing that matters is what you think. That's it. I went through this with Roger in both of our communities. Oh, yeah," Annie assured her, seeing Liz's disbelief, "we were from Benton and Pearse, alright, but we were still considered foreigners because we'd defected for a number of years."

Annie made it sound like such thinking was perfectly normal. Then she reached to smooth her hair down after a gust of wind ran through the field, and she grinned impishly at her friend. Liz laughed out loud.

"You can laugh," Annie said, serious again, "but for all the great things about little towns—and Benton's a great little town—there are things I would love to change. First and foremost? That everyone's welcome, there are no outsiders."

The two started for their bleacher seats but not before Liz tripped and the last of her soda went flying. Very little landed on Mary Sue.

Benton won in overtime with a touchdown and the community celebrated in the cold, clear night. Liz had hoped to see Jay at the game but instead gathered her kids and went home. After putting them to bed, she settled down in front of the fireplace to read a theme paper from twenty years earlier.

7

While the purpose of this paper is to discuss possible career choices for myself once I graduate from Benton High School and from college, that's a pretty tough assignment to write.

Instead, I plan to tell about the choices I will not make. By narrowing down my choices this way I hope I can figure out what I want to do by sorting off what I do not want to do.

Since I was very young, living on a ranch has meant everything to me. It's defined me. I'm that ranch kid who lives a mile from town in a house with a red door, a red door my mother once painted because I came home crying after the second day of kindergarten.

It seems everyone in class could give their street address or some distinctive feature about their rural home except me. So Mom painted the front door red and after that we were the talk of the town.

Our house is only the center of our universe. Our universe is every pasture, hill, tree, corral and outbuilding on our place. I live here along with my older brother, younger sister, our parents and all of the horses, cows, pheasants, wild turkeys, bull snakes, prairie chickens, grouse, mule deer, and coyote.

I have played here, fought here, worked here, and dreamt here. I've learned everything that will ever matter to me right here.

Sometimes I struggle in high school with my feelings and have my family to fall back on. I cannot imagine how the person who grows up without this sense of who they are and what they stand for survives.

In our business we put a brand on the side of an animal to claim it so that thieves can't steal it easily or sell it legally. I think we brand ourselves, too.

We can't ever really leave this place, not totally anyway. I've seen several older ranch kids graduate from Benton and go on to college and careers. Few return to their home ranches for a lot of reasons.

But nearly all of them come back home for class reunions or weddings or the fall festival. They tell all of us how good we've got it. They seem to miss just about everything about this community.

While I don't know what I want to do later in life, I know how I want to feel. I want to feel safe, happy, and loved like I've felt all my life here.

I don't want to settle for an ounce less and I don't want to ask for an ounce more than what I truly need.

I've watched my parents together since I was a young boy. Their hugs and special looks have made me appreciate a good relationship and I know I want to feel like they do about my life partner.

As for work, I suppose it will have to be something with my hands. That's all I've ever done on our place. Being outside in the sunshine and wind and rain has spoiled me into wanting to be unbound forever.

Naturally I'll make use of my math skills and probably do something in the building trade. But for me to sit here and write about my future career is pretty meaningless at this point in my life due to the many uncertainties I feel right now.

As for what I won't do: I won't sell out; I won't become something that I couldn't look at in the mirror and respect; I won't do something just for money.

I'll never be afraid to take a chance and I'll admit my mistakes when I make them. I won't quit making mistakes either.

Oh, and one last won't; I won't ever forget how lucky I was to be born here, into this family, in this part of the world where everyone watches out for me, tells my folks when I egg Mr. Barnady's car on Halloween, and supports me with their hands and their prayers.

> Jay M. Robbins
> 11th Grade English
> 3rd Period

Mrs. Fenton, you probably won't let me get by with this for my theme paper on my future career. But if you do, I'd sure appreciate it.

The clock above the mantle was ticking, keeping a strange cacophonic beat with the crackling logs beside her. Alone with her thoughts, Liz tried to imagine having grown up here, getting to know the landscape and the foibles of the people as well as she knew herself.

She'd thought she was coming to know Benton, and Jay. But this paper written by a sixteen-year-old boy years ago was a window into who he was today. His paper took her back in time, as well, to her own younger years when she had less haze murking up her vision of a good life.

He doesn't care what I do, she realized. But he cares very much, in a way that I've experienced very little before, that I share my life with him.

To Mike, intimacy meant physical closeness. To Jay, it means what I finally discovered I was missing all along—emotional, maybe even spiritual, closeness. Caring for the other person above and beyond my own needs.

The coals were glowing softly when she fell asleep on the floor. She woke a few hours later to the sound of Sugar growling on the porch, troubled by the sound of yipping coyotes.

She rolled to her side, trying to push herself up, and gave out a low moan when her body wouldn't cooperate.

"Just a second." She turned sharply toward a sleep-edged voice and saw Jay dragging himself off her sofa, stocking-footed and hair tousled.

Maybe it was a dream, but Liz could swear she felt hands on her arms. He gently rolled her to a sitting position, too tired to notice her bewilderment.

He pulled her up, letting her down slowly where he'd been lying moments before. He sat on the floor in front of her, studying her.

Poking at the papers laying beside her blanket, like a primitive stirring the remains of an ancient fire, he lifted his eyes to her. "Interesting reading?" His face showed nothing of his thoughts.

"Annie found those in her classroom and gave them to me tonight before the ball game," she mumbled, rubbing her eyes. "A reading assignment, she called it." Liz was frightened of her footing. This was clearly worse than when they'd first met.

"And?"

"And the man who wrote that paper will have crystal relationships all of his life because he won't settle for less." Afraid if she didn't say now what she needed to say, she never would, Liz rushed on.

"I'm not going to sit here, Jay, and alibi how I handled going to Minneapolis the other day. I should have reached you, somehow, before I left and told you what I was doing. At the same time, I don't feel I owe you or anyone else any kind of explanation about anything." She bit her lip and looked down at her hands, gripped tightly together.

Sugar barked sharply. Jay glanced toward the porch, then rose and let the dog into the mud room.

Shutting the door behind himself, he returned quietly to his place on the floor and rubbed his stubbled chin, waiting for her to go on.

"I don't owe you anything," Liz stated more firmly. "You said so yourself and I'm trying to take you at your word." Feeling a draft, she shivered and reached for the throw. Jay tossed it up to her. She kept talking, deciding it would be easier to do so than to listen to the tick of the clock as it marched her heart deeper into her throat.

"I'm not quite sure what to do here, Jay. I feel this expectation from you, this desire to care for me and I'm not ready for that. I suppose that I'm needing time to feel whole before I can think about halving myself for someone again."

She was fairly well embarrassed now. "You could jump in anytime. I feel like I'm really hanging out here," she finished awkwardly, her gaze averted. For a professional woman, she thought, you sound, and look, like an idiot.

"I know what you mean," he agreed, speaking softly. Liz's eyes lifted. "I've been kind of hanging out here myself since Monday, calling myself every kind of name, thinking I'd misread us, feeling like a fool for chasing a woman all over Benton who wasn't interested in the chase. I was mad as hell when I showed up here Monday night and you were gone. To Minneapolis. For a job. I was just another one of the cowboys and you were heading back to the bright lights."

Jay frowned now. "Kent asked me a pretty funny question the other morning. He wondered if I'd drop everything, give up all I was building here and move to Minneapolis for you. And you know what, darlin'?"

He studied her, noticed a tear forming in her eye. "That set me straight." He leaned forward taking a corner of the throw, and dabbed at the drops on her cheek.

"'Course it took me this whole week to realize there's more going on in your life and my life than the other knows or understands. I think we've just got to get past this and go on. By the way," he reached for Liz's hand, playing with her fingers, "I had to do the paper Mrs. Fenton had assigned after all. I wonder why she kept this one?"

"Because she was a woman," she said without thinking. "Because any woman on earth would want to be the object of attention of someone like that."

Encouraged, Jay spoke quickly. "I need to slow down. I know it. Going to church with you and the kids did me in. It felt so natural I forgot where we were." Raising an eyebrow, Jay chuckled. "You know, this would be the part in the movie when the man and the woman walk to the bedroom."

She pulled her hand away, stunned. "But," amused at her reaction, "I wouldn't do that and I don't think you would either. That's just sex until there's a real connection between two people. And if there's a real connection between two people, then the other isn't so damn important as people would have you believe."

"Oh, I think it's a pretty wonderful deal," he said, playfully tugging her hand again, "but not as important as the rest. So what do you say? Proceed at our own pace? "

She quickly processed his changeling comments. "I was just thinking," Liz said quietly.

"What?"

"I honestly don't think you've moved very far from that sixteen-year-old-boy in your paper. I wonder how many people can say that?" Liz leaned forward on the sofa.

She felt her heart beating steadily, hopefully. "Now I'd like to share with you what I was doing in Minneapolis. Not because I owe you any explanation but because I wanted to tell you all along. I just didn't have the opportunity."

Liz told him about the call from her boss after she'd left Jay and Patrick in the park. "I had to make arrangements right away. He and his work group want me to come back to work, but this time out of my home. They offered to send me equipment and projects. I wanted to work out a contract before Kevin could change his mind. To be in front of his desk just like any other early Tuesday morning in the past, rearing to go. I couldn't let this opportunity slip away. It means I can work part time at the store which I truly enjoy, work part-time at home in my old field, and," realizing she needed to say this last piece, "I can still spend time with my kids and..." she paused only fractionally, "with you. "

He rose swiftly and eased himself down by her side, trying not to bump her into more pain. "I'm going to ask you to marry me one day, Liz." She gasped. "And I fully expect you to think I'm nuts for saying that," he nodded. "But that way you'll know where it is I'm heading."

He sat with his elbows on his knees, looking at her carefully. "If you aren't interested at all in that possibility you'd better tell me now, although it probably wouldn't do any good." He laughed heartily and her lips curved upward despite her shock at his words. "I'd probably pursue you anyway. But at least you've got fair warning of where I'm heading."

"I don't believe you," she said, but there was no bite to her words. "Sitting here calmly discussing away centuries of male-female sexual tension and then you make an inane announcement like that. And now we just, what? Discuss what to do with the kids this week?"

Jay's eyes held hers. "Yeah, something like that. I just want you to know I'm not playing around. I care for you. I'll give you plenty of time to decide what you want in your future and I won't bring it up again. As for next week?"

He leaned back and stretched his tired back. He'd lined up help for Kent's harvest and had found a couple neighbors to help wean calves starting in the morning. Lisa would be bringing the three Robbins kids back Sunday afternoon, and he was going to find someone else to keep them.

Liz offered to keep the kids a little longer. "We're so close to their home that we can run over there whenever they need something."

He reluctantly agreed. "Okay. For now. I've really got to get some work done on the complex project this week, so I'm going to hole up at my place. Could you talk to Ben and let him know he can still come over? I'll have some odd jobs for him, but for now I'm concentrating on my project plans. That's my week. How 'bout yours?"

"Just mommying and the Dirt Store and setting up an office here when they get my equipment shipped from Minneapolis. I'm going to leave my computer here in the living room and make some office space in my bedroom for Source equipment."

Jay offered help when that time came and she accepted. "In case you're wondering how I ended up here on your sofa, I was driving home late from the ranch. I saw your lights on all over downstairs so I stopped to check on you. Guess I decided to stick around…make sure you were okay."

Liz touched his sleeve. "I'm glad you did. And, I'm glad we talked. I like how straight forward you are. It's been a long time since I was around someone who was like that with me."

His look was warm, steady. "Liz, we're just a couple of people learning about each other. If you brush away all that social stuff between people, that's really all that happens between a man and a woman when they meet. Just getting to know each other."

Jay rubbed his jaw. He needed some more sleep. "Mind if I finish the night off here? All I need is this blanket and the sofa. I'll be gone early to start weaning."

She said he could stay the rest of the night. "I can make you some breakfast before you go."

He turned her down, saying she didn't need to get up that early. He'd just call her later in the day to see how she was feeling.

"Jay, tonight at the game I overheard a conversation about us."

He scowled.

She'd thought so. "So I imagine I'll be the topic of a few such things if I'm seen with you?"

"Not if, when. And yes, I'm afraid you will. You and I could see each other in Atlanta or San Antonio and no one would know. Here? Everybody, and I mean everybody, knows. It's not the same as the rich and famous, but the same idea. We're the current news in Benton, Liz. That's just how it is in small towns. And we'll be front page until they tire of us or we do something normal like get married and start having kids."

Then he swiftly stood. "I'm sorry. That was stupid." She frowned at this and struggled to her feet, taking his hand when he reached out to balance her. "Pretty insensitive to assume you would want more children," he mumbled, searching for a place to look.

She took both of his hands in hers. "Why don't we save that topic for another conversation, Jay. See you in the morning."

His gaze followed her as she walked to her bedroom and quietly shut the door.

A few hours later, before the sun rose on what promised to be a cold and frosty day, he awakened to the smell of bacon and strong coffee. He lay on the sofa a few minutes, arms under his head, and savored the memories those smells resurrected. Then Jay pulled on his boots and stepped into the kitchen.

An empty coffee mug sat on the counter. He poured himself a cup and turned the bacon in the frying pan. Opening the porch door, Jay saw Liz sitting outside on the top step. Wearing a bulky turtleneck, jeans, and thick socks, she was cupping a steaming mug of coffee.

He pushed open the storm door and sauntered into the still, November morning. Liz turned at the sound.

"Mornin'," he said, tipping his mug toward her. "Good coffee."

"I've had to learn to make it differently here. So many people around Benton seem to like it standing straight up." She moved to the side to make room for him. Together they watched the first rays begin their trek across the morning sky. An owl bid the night farewell as Sugar got an early start on her daily ritual of flushing birds off the ground and rabbits from her territory.

"I turned the bacon. Thanks for the memories." She tilted her head, her eyes questioning. "The smells. It was like when I was a kid and I could smell Mom cooking early in the morning."

"Hmm," she said, nodding, and took another sip. "Jay, I've been sitting here, thinking."

Jay cupped his hands around the mug to warm his chilling hands and watched the rays reach up higher on the horizon. Sugar ran past their vantage point, excitedly sniffing out a rabbit's scent.

"I was so angry with you ignoring me all this week," Liz said, staring across the road. "Angrier than at how you treated me when I got back from Minneapolis. And the coy part of me," she confessed, "would never in a million years admit that. But the part of me that really responds to Benton and to everything around here—that part—really liked how you just said it like you saw it."

She squared her shoulders as she faced Jay. "I am not ready for what you say you are ready for," she barely paused, "but I like what I see."

He touched her hair, then brushed her cheek with the palm of his hand. "When you're ready, let me know." He nodded at their view beyond the steps, over pastures, and to the hills to the east. Morning mist was rising from the frost as sunlight burned off the old and welcomed in the fresh day.

"There's something special about places like this," he said quietly, catching her eye. "I can tell you're responding to the country life. It helps people see what's real, say what they mean."

"I know," she agreed. She rose and went in to make some toast.

He joined her at the counter. They sat munching toast and bacon and drinking their coffee. Tires braked on pavement as a pickup with headlights on turned in Liz's lane and parked by the pickup and car already there. Jay stepped to the window and frowned. "Sorry, Liz, I meant to get an early start. Not early enough, I guess." He walked to the door.

Liz looked out to see what he meant and saw Frank Mundi walking up the steps. Steve Johnson remained in the pickup. Jay stepped out onto the porch to give instructions.

"Saw your rig here," Frank told him, "so I figured I'd stop in and get your orders."

Liz cleaned up the kitchen and went upstairs to wake the kids. She had to leave for work early and had put their breakfast in the oven. "Make sure you're ready by the time I come back for you, about nine," she told them, then went to put on her hiking boots.

She drew on a sweatshirt and coat and picked up her keys and backpack, stepping out into the cold air once again. "Good morning, Frank."

He tipped his brim. "Mornin' Liz."

She turned to Jay. "I've got to get to town early this morning. I'm helping Arch and Ruby with fall cleaning now that things are slowed down. Good luck with your work today. And be careful, will you?" She walked down the steps and to her car.

"I'll call you later," Jay shouted above her car's engine. She waved and drove off.

8

The three men drove north up the gravel road in two pickups, turning in at Kent's place. Saddling horses was the first order of business. Warming bits with their breath, they were climbing on the frisking geldings in short time, stopping only to feed the corralled herd bulls.

"Your brother sure has a good lookin' set of bulls this year," Frank commented as the breeding bulls came up to eat. Jay looked over at the Hereford bulls and nodded agreement. They were a powerful, athletic pair of breeding stock. Bred for their ability to travel well on all terrains and noted for both strong maternal traits and tenderness and flavor of meat in their offspring, the bulls stood side by side at the bunk, eating the grain.

Setting gates along the way, the men left the lodge pole corrals and made their way out to the first of several pastures they would clear that day.

In some places the trail narrowed when it passed through canyons covered with cedar trees. Here they rode single file. Once Jay saw two deer, both older bucks, before the riders fully crested a hill. He watched as the deer bounded away, anxious to stay clear of human contact.

Frank and Steve exchanged work with Kent nearly every year, helping each other with the fall weaning and spring turnout. As ranching got meaner on their cash flows, they let go of their hired men and let some things slide.

Even as they tightened their belts another cinch, they didn't let up on the care of their cattle, their fences, or on the maintenance work that had to be done around their ranches.

They weren't driving new pickups or cars, and their machinery and tractors were older than some of the parts men in the local implement dealerships. Holding on was the common theme at every ranch in the region, let alone in the state. Too many years of work and financial stress were taking their toll on everyone.

But this day the joy of riding a good horse and working with good cattle would shove the negatives of the business to the background. The men snugged down their hats and set to work.

The first pasture of cow and calf pairs splintered off into several different directions when they sighted the horsemen. Jay galloped north after one group of cows and their calves. Frank and Steve headed off to the south to circle twenty, maybe twenty-five pair and point them in the general direction of the pasture corrals.

The two men gradually worked their cattle toward the corral, picking up several singles and pairs along the way. Jay saw to small bunches, twice having to let a cow back so she would bring her calf along with the group.

After nearly an hour, sixty-two cows and their calves were in the central pasture corral. The horses now got a breather; not so for the men.

On foot they sorted calves from cows. Bawling, dust, and hollering filled the air. Jay was kicked a few times and once was knocked flat on the ground by a wild-eyed cow. Not working with cattle on a daily basis was taking it's toll on him.

Brushing off his shirt as he slowly regained his footing, Jay disgustedly reminded himself to read the cow signs and watch the subtle movement of their ears and eyes.

"Some time since you weaned, Jay?" was all Frank said. It's all he had to say. His and Steve's grins across the backs of the cows were an additional motivation for Jay to concentrate harder.

Once the pairs were separated off, the cows were moved out to one fenced-in trap and the calves to a similar pen in the opposite direction. Frank suffered a well- aimed kick by a strapping steer calf. His string of cuss words was well directed, as the calf's mama had blown by all of them earlier, not just once, but twice.

Jay sent a silent note of thanks to his brother on two accounts. The herd bulls had been pulled immediately following the breeding season and wouldn't be in the way today. And Kent maintained good fence lines and corrals.

They may be old; they may be wired together in places and tied with rope in others. But
they were plenty solid. The three wouldn't be
wasting valuable time on carpentry or chasing in
busted out cattle.

When they finished the group, Jay called a
halt. They took a few minutes to wipe sweat
from their faces and to drink the pure water running from the windmill pipe into the huge,
seemingly bottomless tank.

"Good game last night, Jay. You make it?"
Steve asked. His son was the starting quarterback.

"No, I was working on my house and then
ran out to Kent's to do some book work."

Frank and Steve debated the defensive line
assignments briefly. Then the three men untied
their horses and headed to the next pasture a
half-mile away.

Repeating this same gather-and-sort dance,
they worked through the noon hour and into the
afternoon. A few ornery cows and several calves
tested the men's strength and agility and landed
them kicks, bruises, and a couple hoof-on-foot
combinations.

The men were anxious to keep going. The
weather was holding, the cattle were sorting well
enough, and they had plenty of work waiting for
them at home.

Despite the chill in the wind, they shed a
layer of clothing by mid-morning and now were
working in light jackets, their work coats tied to
the back of their saddles.

Jay had grown up helping with the fall weaning work. He'd forgotten how long the day, how big the calves, how stubborn the cows, and just how thirsty, achingly tired, and sore a real cowboy got.

He'd also forgotten how much pleasure came from a bone wearying day when one's progress could be gauged right there before one's eyes. There was a beginning, a middle, and a definite end to the job. Few jobs held such an immediate outcome, he thought, absently rubbing a bruised forearm.

At another break, Frank told them he didn't know if he'd make it this year. "Nothing I've got is worth enough. I raised corn and soybeans. Got calves to sell either now or after the first of the year. None of it is good. Even with some price recovery on the feeder calves, I won't make a profit. Just more than last year."

Steve remained silent. Jay wondered if things were any better at the Johnson ranch, or if it was just too painful for Steve to voice his fears. He knew Kent's family was shaving down every business and personal expense they could, just like they had for each of the past several years.

And he knew his brother had been sleeping poorly, most likely over cash flow worries and paying the operating note off at the bank. With three kids and plenty of debt, his brother had told him shortly before the accident that he didn't know if he could keep operating this way. The lack of real markets and poor public policy which favored large enterprises were killing his business and that of everyone else he knew.

By four they'd finished five pasture groups. Jay and Steve had left for the home corrals midway through the last sort and were returning with pickups and trailers just as Frank pushed the last few calves through the holding pasture gate. Next they began loading.

Now several loads of bawling calves were being driven out of the pasture and unloaded to fill the corrals at Kent and Bonnie's place.

The cows were left out in the pasture where they would also bawl but would likely stay put. Jay remembered the time his father had tried to work the job in reverse; cows to the corrals and calves left out in the pasture pens. It had been a disaster. Cows plowed through fences to get back to the last place they'd mothered their young.

The Robbinses had learned the hard way how cows thought. From that year on, they left the cows where they had last seen their calves. As long as the corrals at home were strong enough, the calves would stay put.

The men finally quit, tired and cold and well past hungry. Typically Bonnie would have packed a lunch but Jay had forgotten to see to this detail.

He asked if Steve and Frank could come again and help him finish the job. "How about Monday? Can you spare another day and we'll finish up those four big pastures over west?"

They discussed the weather reports and how they would go about gathering the larger pastures that remained. After the men spread fresh hay in the bunks for the weaned calves and checked the watering tanks, they called it a day.

Sunday would be a pleasant break for all of them. They agreed to meet at the same place early Monday, and parted, pleased with what they'd accomplished and ready for long, steaming showers.

Liz had put in a big day, as well. She'd waited on a steady stream of customers, finally breaking for a late lunch with the Morrisons in their back office. Arch poked gentle fun at Liz.

He called her their popular employee. "Sure been a lot of new faces in here today, Ruby. Why do you think that is?"

"Now Arch, you mind your own business and pass me that coffee," Ruby said, reproaching him.

Liz frowned, puzzled by his comment and Ruby's response to it. She'd thought it strange so many women had suddenly taken an interest in the correct way to work the earth for plantings next spring or who were wanting her recommendations on garden mulches. "What are you saying, Arch?" He looked up innocently. "Okay, out with it. What's going on?"

"Well, it's like this, Liz. You're new to town, and..."

"New?" she cut in, "I've been here for over six months!"

He chuckled and shook his head. "By Benton's standards I'm new and I've lived here over fifty years. Anyway," Arch continued, warming to his story, "what I'm saying is your seeing that young Robbins feller has everyone curious about just who this Liz Daniels is."

He set his coffee cup on the floor next to his chair and grinned in Liz's direction. "Before? You were a curiosity. You were from out of state. Big city gal. But now you're seeing one of our own. Small places like this are real protective of their people. I'm kind of curious, too," he added, winking at Ruby.

The front door bell sounded, signaling a customer. "Jay's never really shown the kind of interest in anyone here or anywhere else that he's shown in you." He got up and walked out to the front.

Liz turned to Ruby, her mouth wide open. "I'm being analyzed as a potential Mrs. Robbins?"

Ruby laughed and patted her hand. "It could be worse, Liz. They could be plotting to throw a monkey wrench between the two of you. From the comments I'm hearing around town, most people are simply curious about how quickly you two seem to be moving toward one another."

They could hear two voices beginning to argue. Ruby continued, "Remember, honey, Jay's been working these nice, important jobs all over the country. He came home often enough to visit and once in a while he'd bring a woman friend. So people have kept up with him pretty well."

Ruby reached for her napkin and dabbed at her mouth. "Now all of a sudden, after he's been here almost a year, the two of you are linked together in people's minds. I bet it wasn't but a couple hours after church let out that most everyone heard you two were there and looking really comfortable."

Liz's eyes opened even wider, amazed at the undercurrents taking place around her, and she with no idea. Ruby reached down for Arch's coffee cup and Liz hurried to hand it to her.

Ruby took it with a smile of thanks. "That's just how Benton is, and most other small communities where people know one another. Jay and his family are their own people, and they know their mind. He's obviously taken with you, and it looks to me like you're reciprocating."

Liz stood up. Sunlight filtered through the back room window and onto the work bench cluttered with pruning scissors, potting soil, and tools. It framed Ruby, as well.

"It's kind of difficult to live in a fish bowl sometimes, isn't it?" Ruby said, tilting her head as she studied Liz. "It takes some getting used to. On the other hand, there's nothing quite like a fish bowl when you need other people. They know you're in need and they're at your side in a minute. I'd give a bit of advice if you wouldn't mind."

Liz laid a hand on Ruby's arm. "Please."

"Forget about us. All of us. We're just bystanders. This is your life, and Jay's. Live it and don't be influenced by us." They walked out to greet Wayne Darber, who was in his monthly heated discussion with Arch over the school board meeting.

℅

It was 6:30. Liz was about to lock up when the phone rang. "Hello, Dirt Store."

"Hi."

Her pulse spiked at the sound of Jay's voice. "Hi," she answered.

"Are you about done?"

"I am . I was getting ready to head out. The Morrisons took off earlier for a potluck and cards and I was just locking up."

"We're finished here, too. I wondered if you'd like to meet me and get something to eat. I'm coming into town to clean up and I could meet you at the steak house at about, say..." he must have glanced at his watch, "seven?"

She hesitated only a second. "Sure, I'd like that. See you then. "

His hair was still wet and his face freshly shaven when he entered Ginger's Fine Dining. He saw Liz seated at a table with two bachelors from the area. Stopping at the bar, he ordered a beer.

The men were obviously enjoying their conversation. When Liz looked over and noticed Jay she waved him over. He picked up his bottle and walked to the table.

Just jeans and a button down shirt, she told herself. So why is it he looks so great, so much more interesting than any of the men she'd worked with over the years? Or was it who he was and how she was responding to him that made the difference?

The three men exchanged local news and their weaning progress. As soon as Jay sat down, the other two stood and excused themselves, sauntering to the bar.

"Where are Ben and the girls tonight?" he began.

"Annie and Roger took them to Kearney for a movie."

"You paused on the phone when I mentioned coming here," he observed casually as he studied the menu. Then he raised his eyes to see her response.

"I suppose I'm going to have to draw on past experiences of being a duck out of water." Her comment puzzled him until he caught her scanning the restaurant patrons.

"Well, there's one thing you can count on, Liz," pulling her chair closer to his, the legs making a scraping sound on the linoleum.

Jay left his hands on each armrest and looked solemnly into her hesitant eyes. Her hands fidgeted. "Frank and Steve won't add to the rumor mill. They don't care what they saw this morning and they forgot it as soon as we left. They won't give a moment's thought to what they think I was doing at your place at that time of morning."

Two small circles of rosy red spread on her cheeks. Jay sat back and spoke gently, "I do believe you become more conventional by the week, Ms. Daniels."

She blushed deeper. "I know. I said the same thing to Annie weeks ago. Maybe it's the agriculture thing where the guy ropes the cows and women hang out the wash."

She drank from her beer. "Yet, the younger women I know here are anything but conventional. Not many of the older women, either. Quite a few, like Bonnie, work alongside their husbands outside. And others bring home cash from one or two jobs."

Jay picked up his menu again. "Don't be deceived by how simple it all looks. Life is complicated wherever you live it. If it looks too good to be true," he smiled.

Nodding to a corner of the room at a couple in their thirties: "See the two sitting near the second window?" She looked where he indicated. The couple was sitting close together and holding hands.

Jay continued in a low voice. "They're working their way back into a marriage. He started messing around and then I guess she decided to do the same. For a few years they provided more than their share of wild stories for Benton. But they've got a couple little kids and must have decided to take another stab at it. And over there, at the table by the big plant."

He gestured at another couple nearly 60 years old. "They have a wild marriage. They love each other all right, but seem to have trouble remembering it." He watched her look around the room again. Couples, young families, and a few widows were dining.

"All kinds of stories are in this room," Jay said, "just like there were in your neighborhood in Minneapolis or mine in Dallas or Tucson. We just didn't hear them."

He leaned in close, talking slightly above the music from the juke box. "Sometimes you've got to pretend they're not out there. No one but the two of us. It's fine to have a community to kind of keep you on the straight and narrow," his grin was purely devilish, "but no one belongs inside a circle of two but the two, or inside the family's home but the family. After I met Darlene, I knew you'd already learned that one. You'd have had to, Liz. You're too damn smart not to have seen the damage someone like that can do in others' lives."

The waitress finally arrived, apologizing for their wait. "This place is really busy tonight, isn't it?" Liz commented.

The teenager glanced at her gratefully. "It's been crazy all night," she said.

"Must be the cold," Jay said. "Everyone who's been outside just wants to come in and get warm, take their mind off it." They enjoyed their meal and visited, Liz gradually becoming oblivious to their surroundings.

ℰℭ

A few days later Annie and Liz were hiking on Robbins land above the Red Door. The day was far from warm but with a few layers of clothing and by keeping a brisk pace, they were enjoying the breathtaking view. For miles around they could see grasslands, tree belts, livestock watering tanks and the windmills that filled them. Back toward town, the water tower was visible above Benton's tree line.

Standing near the top of a hill about a mile from Liz's home, the two were resting against a fence line corner brace, protected from the stiff wind by a handful of cedar and pine trees. Liz reached for the small water bottle she'd thought to bring along and took a sip, offering a drink to Annie who shrugged it off.

"Thanks, Lizzie. I think I'm going to just shrink a little today. With all these meals I keep eating with Roger, I'm going to be popping out of my clothes soon."

Liz was amused at the thought of her trim friend gaining weight.

Out of the corner of her eye she saw a hawk glide overhead. Suddenly it dove, sighting a field mouse or some other prey, and flew out of sight behind the next hill.

"So tell me, what's up with you and Jay?"

Liz turned back to Annie. "I'd better be getting back before too long or the kids will wonder why we're gone so long."

"Sure, let's go," Annie agreed. "But I still want to hear about the two of you."

Liz struggled with a response. "I really don't know how to answer you. We see each other. We've gone out to eat. I'm taking care of his niece and nephews for a couple more days. He's attracted to me."

"You're attracted to him," Annie interjected.

"Yeah, I am," Liz admitted. "He's a nice, decent man."

Annie stopped Liz at the edge of the steep part of the path. "Nice, decent man, but?"

"But," Liz sighed, her words tumbling out, "I don't want this. I'm just now feeling better, feeling whole. I'm not ready to attach myself to anyone, maybe never again."

Annie shook her head in disgust. "Elizabeth Daniels. Can't you just date someone and quit worrying about ten years down the road?" Annie took a couple steps down the path, then swung around angrily.

"He's a great date!" Annie yelled. "For once would you stop making everything so horribly serious? This is Jay Robbins we're talking about. Any woman would love to go out with the guy. And he wants you!"

"I can't," Liz said, her voice small. She stared at Annie, tears in her eyes. "It's not that I wouldn't like to just quit with the " what ifs". But there's a piece of me inside that keeps saying 'remember what happened the last time you let yourself go and how that all worked out?'"

Before Annie could respond, Liz said, "I know, I know. And I'm working on it. But you haven't been down my road. You don't know how terrifying it is to even consider trusting someone that much again."

She started down the trail. "It's just so funny in a not ha-ha way. I'm trying to accept this man despite swearing off relationships. And as soon as we're apart, all the self doubts come piling in on top of me and it's like, I can't breath."

Her gaze took in the view below them. Snow, settled up against the north sides of tree trunks, lent a holiday air to the setting. The tracks of a rabbit careened off to the left, the trail several hours old. Liz somehow felt a part of this chilly scene.

"I'm working on it, Annie. I just don't have a pat answer for your 'how's it going?'" She looked at her watch. "Now we've really got to get moving."

෪෮

Arch took off early the next day for his monthly game of poker with his coffee buddies. Ruby asked Liz if she and her kids would like to join her for an early supper. Liz happily accepted. Spending time with Ruby was like curling up in an overstuffed chair, a favorite book in hand.

Liz had offered to help with the meal but Ruby had said she was making something simple and not to bother. After they closed the store, Liz drove out to the Red Door and picked up her children.

Entering Ruby's back door, they were met by the most tantalizing aroma. Liz could tell a stew had been cooking all day, filling the house with wonderful smells. They found Ruby in the kitchen.

A few minutes later they were sitting around the Morrisons' dining room table. "Oh, Ruby, this is so good," Liz raved. "What's in it?"

Ruby smiled and passed Ben a basket of biscuits and a bowl of wild grape jelly. "Oh, it's just something I throw together. I don't even have a recipe. I just do what my mother did, and add a few things here and there. Kind of make it with whatever I have on hand, you know."

They visited about the Dirt Store, Arch's card playing cronies, and the cold weather. After the kids finished and went downstairs to the game room, Ruby asked Liz about Jay.

"A few weeks ago," Liz answered thoughtfully, "I knew I didn't want to see him. I just wanted to live quietly, move on with my life. But I think I have this choice to make, this intersection in the road, and he is one of the directions." She studied Ruby. "How well do you know him?"

"Jay? I suppose I've known him since he was a little boy. I knew his mother very well. I think he dated one of my older granddaughters for a while when they were in high school."

"The reason I asked," Liz said softly, "is he's not real easy to put off."

Ruby chortled at that. "Liz, he's a Robbins," as if that explained it. "They are marvelously fair, good people. They know their own minds and even if they're the only ones in ten thousand who feel a certain way, they still feel that way."

"You know," Liz continued, comfortable in their conversation, despite Ruby's high amusement, "I've noticed that about him. And I like him. I just have to be sure that it's me, and not just him telling me what I think."

Ruby considered Liz's perceptive words and a long ago memory they triggered. "I remember when I met Arch after I came to work here in Benton."

She laughed fetchingly and swept her white hair off her forehead. "I had just graduated from high school and needed a job. Arch and I took one look at each other and that was it."

Ruby smiled at this as she started gathering dishes from the table. Liz hurried to help her, eyes studying Ruby's expressive face. Ruby went on.

"I remember being so scared at how fast everything was happening. How could two people who had just learned one another's names become so close in so short a period of time?" Thinking of it, Ruby brushed her cheek as if her beau had just touched her there.

She opened the dishwasher door and began loading it with glassware. "It wasn't like now, Liz. People didn't have much time alone together. There were all these social rules. And we had so little free time, what with work and our families and all. But his eyes," she said dragging out the word, "they were so intense. And he was funny."

She looked brightly at Liz, her eyes growing larger at another memory. "Arch used to talk to me in a way that told me I was the most important thing in his life." She leaned back against the counter top, sizing up Liz with a sage look. "I think I understand how you feel, honey. I am still amazed after all these years at how Arch and I found our way to one another despite all the eyes on us."

She reached for a plate and paused again. "I've got a secret for you." She twinkled like the eighteen-year-old girl who first came to Benton. "I wasn't going to stay here. It was just a stepping stone for me. I had plans, you see. I wanted to save money and go to college. But," she rinsed the plate and handed it to Liz, "that didn't work out. I'm happy with my life as it is."

She and Liz loaded the rest of the plates and silverware in the dishwasher, and after pouring in soap, Ruby turned it on. They moved to the front room and sat in winged back chairs near a crackling fireplace.

"You've been through a lot, Liz. I wouldn't have the slightest idea how to live through what you've experienced. Maybe it feels like Benton's dishing it out pretty good right now. You being from the city, it's going to be hard to take the invasion of privacy. I'm not going to tell you what to do or how to feel or think. That's for you to figure out. But I do know that when I've listened to my heart, I haven't been wrong too many times." Just listening and questioning Ruby helped Liz through a maze of emotions.

The next weekend Liz and Annie met Jay and Roger at Lots to celebrate Roger's birthday. Choosing a table close to the dance floor, Jay said it would be more convenient, not that they need to dance, but only if they want to dance, he said, looking meaningfully at Liz.

"And leave me sitting here?" Annie pouted. "Either you're going to ask me to dance, Mr. Robbins, or get this good looking hunk of manhood here to do it. I'm not sitting still for one more song!"

Jay grabbed Annie's hand and together they hit the dance floor. Liz and Roger broke into laughter, he quickly setting his drink down before he could spill it.

"Aren't you glad she took him away?" Roger asked when he could get a breath. "Leaves us to a few minutes of sanity."

"Don't you like to dance?" Liz asked, following Annie and Jay's progress around the dance floor.

"Dance? Yes. Engage the whole room? No."

She shook her head in wonder. "Roger, I've known Annie for years. She's always been this totally outlandish person."

"If you know her that well, Liz, then you know why I fell for her."

The song ended. Annie tugged Roger out onto the dance floor next. Jay sat down, took a drink from his beer, and glanced around. "There are a lot of people here tonight," he commented.

Liz kept her eyes on Annie and Roger and nodded her agreement. One of Kent's neighbors stopped by to ask Jay how the calves were doing and when his brother might come home.

A slow waltz began. Jay waited for Liz's eyes to meet his. "It's up to you" he said.

She sat another few seconds, then reached for his hand. "Would you like to dance?"

"I'd like to dance with you."

Leading her to the far side of the dance floor, Jay took her in his arms. They began moving to the ballad and were joined by several more couples.

They kept time with the music and moved about the floor, neither speaking. At the end of the song they stopped, still holding one another, still staring at one another, bound together in the minds of everyone there that night.

9

The days flew by and homework got tougher. The Daniels dining room table was nightly turned into the groan and moan center. It was now the week before Thanksgiving.

Kent had continually surpassed his doctors' expectations, and his condition was routinely upgraded. Therapy was going well. One sure sign of how far Kent had come was how crazy he was feeling cooped up in the hospital.

Anxious to get home didn't come close to describing his anticipation at leaving the antiseptic environment and getting back to his ranch and family. Bonnie had taken to alternating a couple days at the hospital and then a day at home.

The Robbins kids moved back and forth between their home, friends' homes, and their aunt and uncle's in Kearney on weekends. Liz kept offering, and every so often she kept them but Bonnie and Kent felt she'd done more than enough to help them out.

Jay's plans for the office complex were progressing. He had driven to Kearney twice already this week to meet with the investors.

"He's been on the run since he finished up his brother's harvest and cattle work," Liz explained to Annie. "He stops by sometimes at night on his way back from Kent's and we've gone out to eat a few times the past two weeks. He fell asleep the while we were talking on the phone the other night. It was only nine and he was exhausted."

Annie was sitting on the floor, leaning back against the bean bag chair and surveying her friend's face with interest. "So?" Liz looked up. "So what's going on with you two?"

That question again. Liz smiled slowly, warmed by the thoughts the answer evoked in her this time. "I don't know."

""Lizzy," Annie drawled, "I've known you since our freshman year at the University of Nebraska. That smile does not say to me 'I don't know.'"

"You know, sometimes you are incredibly nosy," Liz said. She walked over to the bay window and glanced out to check on Jane and Tess. They'd gone out an hour earlier to play in the new snow.

Annie tried again. "Ever since the second Sunday you two went to church together, the one when all the kids were in Kearney? Ever since then, even the postmaster knows more about your doings than I do. Course, Benton being Benton, I hear about it pretty soon afterwards." Her comment hit the mark.

"You've been so busy planning your wedding you haven't had a minute to think about anything except your job and Roger," Liz said without thinking. She turned away from the window and sat down by the hearth. "I don't blame you, either. You look happier each time I see you." She changed the subject. "So what are you and Roger doing for Thanksgiving?"

"We're going to Arizona to see my parents. We haven't seen each other in months. I guess the last time they were here was a few months before you moved to Benton. They want to spend a little time with us before the wedding. How about you? Any plans yet?"

"Some tentative ones. The kids fly out tomorrow to spend the weekend with Mike. He has a new girlfriend and I imagine she's curious about his kids. Next week Mom and Dad are coming from Minneapolis. It's silly, but Mike and Darlene won't let the kids see my parents while they're in town. You know Darlene..." Liz said.

She stretched her arms above her head and shook her head at the pettiness. "I guess that pretty much cinched Mom and Dad's decision about coming here for the holiday. I invited Jay and Kent and Bonnie's family to come. Bonnie said there was a chance Kent might be out of the hospital by then or at least out for the day. If not, though, she and the kids will spend the day down there."

"Liz, did you know that Gran and Grandad are going to be alone this year? None of Dad's family can get back."

"I'd love to have them. I'll talk to them tomorrow morning. I was planning on going in and doing a little work anyway. I've hit a lull with my public relations work. Nothing's happening over the holiday."

A snowball hit the window, sending Liz outdoors to track down the offender. Ben had reappeared just in time to start a snowball war. Annie was peppered when she left a few minutes later, and although Ben was properly dealt with, Liz knew it would only correct his mischievous behavior, not his outlook.

He's a lot like Jay, she realized. That's probably why they enjoy one another so much. She ducked and went back in the house as Jane's attempt to imitate her brother was off by roughly ten degrees.

₮℞

The three left for their trip to Minneapolis. After their return, little was said about their visit and it was a few days before they were back to normal. Liz saw this as a pattern that played out after each phone call from Mike. The trip had elicited a similar, though longer lasting, effect.

Jay commented Wednesday on how quiet Ben had been a few days earlier when he'd stopped to help after school. "Was he sick?"

She shook her head. "He's just coming down off of Minneapolis and Mike. It's like they're in a different environment with different expectations. It's a real clash with how we live. I guess they got quite the lecture when Tess mentioned you to Mike. There stood his girlfriend and he was telling the kids how I shouldn't be seeing anyone. Jane told me Ben just looked at his dad and pointed out the irony."

They were rearranging furniture, making space so they could open the dining room table to its full capacity. The Morrisons had accepted her invitation. Kent could leave the hospital for part of Thanksgiving Day, so he and Bonnie and the kids would also be there. Liz's folks were arriving later in the evening, and Liz was nervous.

She had never thought of herself as much of a cook and the thought of preparing for fourteen mouths now seemed an overly ambitious plan. Add to this the thought of introducing Jay to her parents, and Liz's stomach had an odd combination of dread and excitement gurgling in it.

Jay was standing before her, amusement in his eyes. "You sure you don't need me to do anything else? I'd be glad to stay and help."

She knew he was stalling in the hope of meeting her parents. She, on the other hand, was anxious for him to leave. Finally he did, but not without a kiss. A long, drawn out, on fire kiss.

Liz watched him drive off to town. The crisis mode of those first days after Kent's accident had brought her into a unified state with Jay. She knew if she were honest she would have to admit she'd enjoyed these past few weeks. She'd felt like a partner, helping her to ease the fears she'd carried far too long.

ଛଔ

By noon the following day the house was filled with scents of a big family holiday meal.

Softly glowing tapers graced the dinner table, the fireplace mantle, and the kitchen. The television in the corner of the living room drew football enthusiasts or those simply looking for the noisiest crowd.

Arch was there, as were Kent and his boys. Jay had gone after his brother that morning, freeing Bonnie to help Liz in the kitchen.

"Not that I think you need any help, Liz," Bonnie said when she arrived. "Everything looks fabulous! But I remember the first few times I cooked for a big group. A couple extra hands came in pretty handy. Kent and Jay's mom was so good to me."

Ruby was in the kitchen, as was Anita, Liz's mom. Together they were putting the last touches on a relish tray.

Jane had taken Fran upstairs to see the books she'd gotten for her birthday a few days earlier. Tess had tagged along, determined to keep up with the older girls no matter what. Ben was sitting near Jay and Grandpa Raymond, watching the two men interact.

At a break in the conversation, Jay slipped out to the kitchen. He caught Liz on a trip to the fridge and raised his eyebrows. "Kent told me this was the last place I should go today. He said it's kind of out of my league, but I don't know. Sure smells good." He sniffed the air like a ravenous bear circling a bustling campground.

Anita smiled as she handed the now finished tray to him. "What a wonderful find you have here, Liz. A man who isn't afraid of a kitchen. There still aren't enough around. Are you going to be the one carving the turkey?"

Liz knew it was a challenge, this look of Jay's. "Would you mind?" she asked him. "We'll be done here in a few minutes."

Anita smiled knowingly. This man, she liked. He was good for Liz. And Ben was certainly fond of him. She left to wash up as did Ruby. Bonnie left the kitchen to check on Kent and found her sons close by his side.

Jay and Liz were alone for a moment. Setting the tray back on the counter, Jay drew her behind the kitchen wall, and took her face in his hands. Her silky black dress clung to her figure when she moved.

"Thank you," he said, kissing her, then deepening the kiss.

"For what?" she asked, when he stepped back. Her heart was pounding.

"For making my decision to take you to the dance look better all the time."

Raymond stuck his head in the doorway and asked for the wine. Liz handed him two bottles, then reaching for the relish tray, she gave it to Jay and sent him out to the table.

Liz quickly checked the counters, refrigerator, and oven to see if she'd forgotten anything. She came at last to the table with the platter of turkey.

Raymond finished pouring the wine and as soon as Liz took her place, all joined hands and prayed a blessing over the meal and one another. On the amen the kids reached for dishes of food only to be stopped midair by the sound of Kent clearing his throat.

When he had everyone's attention, he raised his glass, clutching his wife's hand as he did so. Liz felt her eyes burn at the look of love in his eyes. Jay, sitting to Liz's side, watched her as he listened to the toast.

"I know there are better ways to get out of doing a little work." Laughter ran around the table. "There's probably no better way of seeing how much people care about you, though, than by what I've been through. Bonnie, you held my hand and got me to this point, and only chewed me out once in a while. And I pretty much had it coming each time."

She threw her dinner napkin at him as he ducked. "Thanks to you I'm here today. You took charge, kept me working at rehab, didn't let anyone get away with less than one hundred and ten percent." He leaned forward to whisper in her ear and wipe away a tear.

"Jay." He stopped and got control of his voice. "You did everything that needed doing and then some. I remember waking up in the hospital the night of the accident and you were there, just like that football coach we had. Remember him? The one we called Coach Holler 'cause that's all he ever did."

There was more laugher at the table before Kent added, "You've always been a good brother. I'll never forget all you've done for us. Thank you."

Jay bowed his head in Kent's direction. Liz squeezed his hand.

"And Ms. Liz." Surprised to hear her name, she looked down the length of the table at Kent.

"You were a stranger to our family a few months ago. Today you are counted among our most cherished friends. You took in our children, and that mutt Sugar." The kids protested loudly here.

"There were plenty of people who did plenty of good things for us these past weeks, but few with the generosity of heart, the amount of time, or the complete disregard for their own personal life like you did. While I lay in that blasted bed all this time, there were two things Bonnie and I didn't have to worry about and they're what's most important to us: our children, and our ranch. I thank you from the bottom of my heart."

All glasses were lifted and just as they began clinking Kent finished. "Now I know why we couldn't rent this place out last spring when ol' Shickley moved on. Had your eyes on this fine woman even then, Jay, didn't you?"

Good natured teasing and laughter filled the house. Jay carved the turkey, helped Liz oversee the first passing of plates, and went out to the kitchen for another bottle of wine.

Ruby had brought her renowned sweet potato dish. Bonnie shared pickled beets and a broccoli casserole. Anita had risen early to bake horn rolls and some kolaches with cherry and apricot fillings. Liz had made her mother's pimento and oyster corn dish.

When the last of the pie plates and coffee cups were cleared, the kids put their heads together to organize a sledding party on the hill above the barn.

Ben was coaxing his grandpa to join them but Raymond was begging off, citing a sudden urge to seek out a quiet corner. The dishes were piled and soaking in the sink. A comfortable lull enveloped the adults.

Now, Jay decided. Walking over to the fireplace he held up his hand for attention. As the last of the conversations died out, Liz stepped from the kitchen to see what was happening. She saw Jay standing in front of everyone.

Then he looked directly at her. The air between them sped up, drawing the space into a continual loop, racing atoms connecting them. She stopped breathing.

"I feel I should say a few words of thanks to Liz for her hospitality. It's been a good day. We had great people at this table, good food on it, and nice conversation around it. I don't believe it gets any better than that. Kent, you were right."

He looked over to where his brother was resting on the sofa, Bonnie's arm around him. "There was method to my madness from the beginning. But now that you've gotten to know her, I think you can understand why we really didn't need to rent this place out last spring."

Liz took a step closer. He's singing you a love sonnet, her heart told her. Don't Jay, her mind countered.

"Anita, Raymond, it's a pleasure to get to know you. I've been wanting to meet Liz's parents and I'm not disappointed." Both of them looked at their daughter, saw her standing so achingly torn between what may be her future and what was her past.

"Arch and Ruby, thanks for having that job opening when she was looking for a place to work. You made it pretty handy for me. Otherwise I'd have had to find her somewhere else, in some other town." He looked back at her, reaching out his hand to her. "And I would have."

It took a bit to get her legs working. She reached his side as he took a box out of his pocket. She panicked at what would be inside.

He held it between them. "Liz, I have a little something here for you." He opened it and drew out a silver necklace and earring set. He clasped the necklace around her neck. "This whole part of the country looks different to me now that you're in it."

He looked at Ben, then Tess and Jane. "You've got the greatest kids in the world. I just wanted to thank you for all you've done for my family." Then he held out the earrings and waited for her to take them, that damned, cocky, gorgeous grin of his plastered across his face.

He would do something like this in front of everybody, Liz thought. His brother and wife were looking on, satisfied. Their children and hers, silent for what may well have been the longest period of their young lives.

Ruby and Arch were smiling their happiness for her. And her parents, he timed this for them particularly. Jay wanted to challenge her, she realized. He wanted her to decide. And he wanted to scare the hell out of her.

She swallowed once, twice, and looked around the dining room. Well, she thought, we'll see about that. "I, I'm not nearly as accomplished a speaker as this guy here," their warm laughter easing her nervousness, "although I do just fine in a work setting. I think I'm a little more private about things than Jay." She gave him a dark look and he only grinned. "However, a big talk like that definitely deserves a response, don't you think?" Ben and Kyle, old enough to follow the pitches and turns of this event, joined the adults in clapping and whistling.

"So here goes. And you know, Jay," she said quietly to him, "I did not have time to prepare my talk."

Yeah, he thought to himself, but you're definitely up to whatever challenge gets thrown at you.

She looked at her parents. "I found out why I gravitated toward this house in the beginning. Jay and Kent's mom painted the door red so that this place would be different, special. I've always thought of it as the Red Door house. She didn't just paint the door. She painted the people in it, put her mark on them. I think that's what we do to people we care for, stamp them with the best we've got in us."

She paused, took a deep breath, and looked at her guests. Her hands were tightly clasped but a smile played about her lips. "When I moved to Benton I was pretty much immune to all the ebbs and flows of a small town. Slowly I've come to understand certain things. I suppose I have a long way to go because the layers, the richness of the rural community and it's inhabitants are amazing. I immediately loved the sounds and colors of this area. Learning about and accepting the rest that goes with this way of life is the real challenge."

She looked directly at the Robbinses. "But you, Kent and Bonnie, welcomed me into your family without a thought. You trusted me with your kids and I know how much they mean to you. It is I who thanks you." Bonnie inclined her head. Kent nodded, enjoying the show.

"Ruby, Arch, you have been wonderful employers and friends. I, too, am glad you had a job when I needed one so I could come to my friend Annie's hometown." Next she looked at her parents.

"Mom and Dad." She laughed outright. "I'll bet you never pictured this daughter here, did you? Maybe Megan or even Teresa, but me? I did the urban stuff. The ballet, the symphony, worked in the city, drove to the soccer tournaments in mom car pools. Me, digging in people's gardens? But I have never felt more comfortable with my life than I feel right now. Thanks for being here, and for always being there for me."

Anita wiped at an eye as her husband blew their daughter a kiss.

She turned back to Jay. Stepping closer, Liz said the first thing that came into her mind. "If you'd really been on the ball, Jay, you could have told me this great place was for rent a little earlier and I could have moved in during the summer when we had more time. Honestly, couldn't you have moved a little quicker?"

The living room erupted in cheers as Jay stared down at her. "You always manage to one-up me, you know that?" he murmured before the kids rushed them, begging him to go sledding.

Caving in to their insistent pleadings, he shouted above the noise. "All right! Meet you out on the porch in your boots, coats, stocking caps, and gloves. Two minutes. Three minutes, tops!"

Liz stepped in front of the mirror by the mud room door to take out her earrings and put in the new pair.

"I got them in Kearney last week. I thought of you the minute I saw them," Jay said as he reached for the door handle.

"They're beautiful. Thank you."

He started to say something, thought better of it, and opened the door. Then he stepped back and looked in the mirror at their joint reflection. "You thought something else was in that box, didn't you?" When she raised her eyes sharply, he only nodded and smiled. "Yeah, I thought so." Then lowering his voice a notch, "I told you what I want, Liz, and that I'll give you time to make up your own mind. I won't push, especially not in front of others."

Then he went out to the mud room to bring some semblance of order, leaving her struggling to remember what her problem was with this relationship and why she couldn't make up her mind about what she wanted.

"Wow, has he ever been roped in." Annie had arrived home from Arizona on Sunday afternoon about the time Liz's parents left, and was now admiring her friend's earrings and necklace. "He really said all of that in front of your parents and his family? And Gran and Grandad? What did your kids think?"

"They thought it was great fun." Then she remembered Annie's comment. "Roped in? Is that what you think?"

Annie made an exaggerated face, and rolled her eyes. "Of course not. I was just thinking about how single he is, that's all. Just like Roger. And me, I suppose. But he's worked all over and didn't seem that interested in the domestic thing."

Annie wiggled her eyebrows at Liz and pulled her coat on. She had promised to help Grandma Ruby with a little project and she was nearly late. "Jay's been the one guy this town has known for years who was everyone's favorite uncle, friend, party-goer. And yet, you can look at him now and wonder how anyone could miss what a great partner he'd make for some fortunate woman."

Liz scrunched her face. "Annie. It's a necklace and earrings."

"No, if there ever was a guy head over heels, it's him. The way you described his little show, I'd say he's hooked." She tweaked Liz's cheek. "Cheer up, sweetie. Just remember how it felt when you two were mad at each other. Wasn't much fun, right? So knock off the complaining about his attention."

She stood up and faced Liz with a shrewd look. "You know, you're going to have to make up your mind. Are you going to live or only look like you're living? Roger and me, we were just dating and then, all of a sudden, we knew we were going to get married. But you and Jay? Honey, that's just pure fate, through and through."

She laughed and held up her arms as if to deflect a flying object. "Don't get mad at me for saying what you're thinking. Just because you're all twisted inside doesn't mean I have to be. I can see what you're feeling and what he's doing. He's giving you all the space in the world and being real patient about it. Just don't take too long."

Annie walked out and left Liz with the sounds of the clock ticking on the mantle. She had an hour before Jay was to pick her up for a date. Too much time.

Throwing on her winter gear, Liz struck out on a quick hike in the hills, reminding the kids to go in before it got dark. She set a fast pace and found herself thinking about Jay most of the way.

Benton had provided her an alternative to what she'd thought she'd have when she arrived, all right. She was looking for peace and quiet, a good school for her kids, different work to take her mind off the past.

She'd found all that, plus a far richer life than she'd expected. She may not know what to do with him, but could she walk away from him?

She was no closer to an answer when she got back to the Red Door. Jay was parking his truck as she jogged up the front stairs. "Forget about me?" he asked, shutting his pickup door.

"Not hardly," she said. "Just lost track of time. I'll be ready soon." He followed her in, she hurrying to her bedroom. "Sit down and read the paper," she said, as he stood so comfortably in her home. "Waste a little time while I hurry." She pulled off her stocking cap and shook out her hair, dropped her coat on the floor, and slammed her door.

His laughter followed her into her bathroom. Jay sat down on the sofa and picked up the Benton Times. Ben came down from his bedroom, glad to see Jay. Tess and Jane heard voices and also came to see who was in their home.

"Something funny?" Jay asked Liz as they left twenty minutes later.

"Actually, I was just wondering what I'm going to be doing tonight." The babysitter had arrived shortly after Liz got out of the shower. Jay had let her in, visiting with her about the basketball team's prospects.

Now as Liz and he walked to his pickup he noticed a grin on her lips. She shrugged off his question and climbed in. "Your orders were to dress warm. So we're not going to a movie or a restaurant. Exactly where are we going?"

Jay started the engine and backed out onto the road. He turned north and drove further away from Benton, pulling into a ranch about five miles west of Kent and Bonnie's place.

Cars, pickups, and other four-wheel drives were parked in rows surrounding the large steel storage shed. Lights from a couple windows welcomed arriving couples, wrapped warm against the late November temperature.

"What's this?" she asked Jay. He took her hand and half ran to the building, the raw wind chasing them to the steel door. Opening it, he pulled her in. She was greeted by the site of several people she knew from the area and by loud country music.

"Did your folks get off in good time today?" Roger asked. Annie laughed at her friend's surprised look. She pointed around the party with her can of soda.

"Isn't this wild? Benton and Pearse have taken turns for years hosting a Thanksgiving dance in somebody's barn or shed. I never miss it when I'm home."

Jay moved off to say hello to an old friend he hadn't seen in years, taking both of their coats with him. Roger went back to sorting through CDs, looking for a selection to satisfy the older crowd.

A few minutes later Jay returned to where Annie and Liz were visiting, two beers in hand. "This is the highlight of the year in both our communities," he explained, handing one to Liz.

"It can get pretty crazy, too," he cautioned, a gleam in his eyes. "No one under twenty-one is allowed. The adults can cut up and their kids can't watch them. Seems to work pretty well. The cutting up part, that is." He nodded at the antics of a couple near the refreshment table.

"Who plans it?" Liz asked, taking in the number of people who were arriving and those already dancing and visiting. For a rural community with miles of roads, people had come from all over to get together for a little fun.

Jay pulled her to the side before she was jostled by a couple who's two-step was expanding in energy by the second. "Each year someone volunteers as host," he said. "Everyone pitches in to help with the food and drinks. And just about every year something happens to make the dance memorable."

The way he said that caused Liz to look at him more closely, but he was glancing around the room, studying the crowd.

A new song began. Jay took her beer and set both their drinks behind some bales of hay. Then he drew her to the center of the dance space. Nearly thirty couples were swaying to the music by the time the song ended. The second and third songs drew another dozen. Then they took a break. Liz spotted Arch and Ruby and walked over to talk.

All of a sudden she heard Jay's voice over the speaker system announcing Roger and Annie's engagement dance. Whistles and applause filled the shed. As if by tacit agreement, everyone moved back when the waltz began, leaving a small circle in the middle where the couple stood. Roger and Annie danced, surrounded by well wishers.

Liz looked at Jay, now understanding his earlier comment. She saw Roger catch Jay's eye, a message passing from one to the other.

Jay climbed down from the stand where the music system was set up and asked Liz if she wanted to eat. They ate and danced, talking with nearly everyone during the course of the evening.

Around one o'clock the party wound down, and tired couples moved out of doors to their cold vehicles. Annie caught Jay and Liz before they left, and invited them to her house for coffee.

The men talked in the kitchen after serving the coffee, leaving Liz and Annie alone in the living room. "You still do that solitaire thing on your computer?" Annie asked.

"Sometimes. Why?"

"I don't know," Annie shrugged. "I guess I thought it was funny that you were fascinated by it. Then I came across a short story I hadn't read in years, probably since I was in high school, and it reminded me of what you said about the game."

"What story?"

"**Bartleby the Scrivener**. The Melville story. Remember it?"

"I don't think I know it, Annie."

Roger stuck his head in the room asking if they needed more coffee. Neither did.

"Well there's this guy," Annie explained, "a scrivener or scribe, who works for this man. He's pretty much stepping back from life, barely functioning. The whole story revolves around his phrase 'I prefer not to'. You come to learn, as the tale unfolds, his not choosing is choosing."

"Anyway," Annie tossed her curly head, yawning hugely, "it reminded me of what you said about how each time you play solitaire, you can make just one different move and the entire result is changed. This Bartleby guy, he plays it the same over and over again. He constantly prefers not to choose and yet that's a choice. So the outcome still is affected by him. He is choosing."

"That is another take on the card game," Liz agreed. She set her cup aside and stood up slowly, suddenly very tired and needing to turn in for the night.

"In what way?" Annie asked.

"In that I don't need to do everything radically different in my life because so many pieces of my life are different now. I suppose I could even do everything the same, be exactly the same person I was in Minneapolis, and the outcome would still be different."

She stopped and stared at Annie.

"Liz? Are you okay?" Annie asked, touching her shoulder. Liz shook her head as if to clear her thinking while she reached for her coat on the back of the sofa. After stepping into the kitchen to ask Jay if he was ready to go, she looked at Annie.

"I was just listening to what I said. I'm not the same person I was two years ago. I think we're all different with different people. Not necessarily acting out roles or trying to be what that person wants. It's just that different things come out of us around different people with different encouragement."

Annie hugged her goodnight. "What did I tell you?" she whispered. "Give him a chance." Annie got louder, as the men walked in. "If my friends in Omaha could see me now they'd laugh themselves silly. I'm not totally altered, but there are different influences on me here. And Roger has been pretty good for me. Kind of quieted me down."

Laughter spilled out of Annie as amazement registered on his face.

"If this is quiet, can you imagine what she was like before I met her?" Roger asked Jay.

"I kind of hate for this evening to end," Jay said later as he drove down the frosty street.

"Me too," Liz said. "Say, I haven't been inside your house in weeks. How's it coming?"

"Want to stop and take a look?"

He parked in the driveway and unlocked the front door, pushing it open. Turning on the lights, Jay took her through the downstairs first, then up the winding staircase to the second story.

"You're almost done. It looks wonderful." She turned around and saw him leaning against the bannister where she'd seen him last summer with Ben. His arms crossed, he was again watching her.

"I was wondering how you're doing with 'us' now?" he asked quietly.

"I'm doing better" she said, studying his features.

He started toward her, then stopped. "I think I'd better get you home. We both have to get going early in the morning which is in about four more hours." She watched him out of the corner of her eye as he drove the mile to her home and pulled into her driveway. "I think I'll just let you off here, Liz."

She got out, aware of his altered behavior. His window slid down as she walked around the front of the pickup.

"I wasn't worried about you in there, Jay. I trust you."

"Yeah, well, that's only one of us." She watched him drive back toward Benton.

10

The morning of Annie and Roger's wedding dawned sunny and beautiful. It was five days before Christmas and the weather was toying with Nebraska; it felt like a premature spring.

Annie called Liz early in the morning and said she was going to the church hall to check a few last minute details. She wanted Liz to meet her at her house in time to go to the church with her.

Now the phone rang and Liz glanced at her clock as she reached for it. The time—10:30—etched into her memory as she heard the hospital nurse identify herself and calmly, clearly tell Liz the reason for her call.

Carefully she replaced the phone. Reaching for her car keys and bag of make-up, Liz pulled on a long wool coat and studied her reflection in her mirror. She saw a woman dressed in a deep blue attendant's gown, eyes staring back from somewhere far away.

A choked cry escaped her, followed by a prolonged, jagged intake of air that had her chest working unevenly. Liz grasped the top of her dresser to steady herself, and staring at her face, willed control. She covered two tear streaks with more make-up and cleaned up her smudged eyeliner.

Calling for the girls and Ben to get their coats, she went through the motions of checking their clothing and hair and sending them out to the car. She drove in silence to town. The kids, picking up on her mood, talked in hushed tones.

When they got to Annie's, Liz took her friend aside. A few minutes later she came back into the living room and told her children to stay put, that she would call as soon as she could.

In a wedding gown and maid of honor attire, the two entered the hospital's emergency entrance and followed the hallway to where Roger was standing.

Moving through a group of family members and stepping inside the room, they walked to a bed now surrounded by beeping and humming machines. Ruby, standing beside Arch's head, a hand holding his, turned now to her granddaughter and friend. She welcomed them into her arms.

"You can give your grandfather a hug, Annie dear." Ruby dabbed at her eyes, tears building all the while. "Then you'd better get to the church. It's nearly time for that big step in your life." Staring at her grandfather, Annie remained as if rooted.

The pain in the room was palpable. Like on a still, hot day in late summertime, Liz struggled to draw breath. She signaled to Roger and taking his and Annie's arms, tugged them to the back of the room.

"They're doing everything they can," Liz whispered. "You know what Arch would want you to do. I'll stay a little while longer, okay?" They nodded and left. Slowly, the rest of Arch and Ruby's family left after first hugging their father, father-in-law, grandfather, uncle.

Liz remembered Jay coming in, touching Arch's motionless hand, offering to pick up Ben and his sisters. Father Bob came to see Arch and Ruby. Still, she remained by Ruby's side, listening with her to the doctor and nurses as they attended to Arch, together trying to understand what was being said.

It was an hour before the wedding and Ruby asked Liz to step out of the room with her. "Thank you for sitting with me. Arch and I've been grateful for you ever since you came to us. You thought it was we who gave you a new start, but you've given us quite a little, too."

Ruby's voice caught. She dabbed her eyes with a tissue and looked through the window at her husband. "Now go to the church for our granddaughter. Tell people that everything's going to be just fine and we'll hope and pray for that."

Not knowing what else to do, Liz hugged her and promised to return as soon as she could. And then she did as she was bid. She rushed to the church and smiled for the camera. She walked down the aisle in front of Annie and handed her Roger's ring. She walked out on Jay's arm and toasted Annie. She danced one dance with Jay and one with Roger.

And then Liz asked one of her babysitters, who was also at the reception, if she'd mind keeping an eye on her children. She slipped out a side door and entered the hospital to find Ruby still sitting by her husband, still holding his hand. But he was gone.

The room was quiet. She could hear the hum of the now useless equipment and the ticking of the clock on the wall. The air. It was so dry, spent. She could tell that death had visited and so she stood in the doorway until Ruby turned her head, a jagged smile on her lips, and beckoned Liz.

She stepped back into the hallway and let go a quick sob, then forced herself to reenter Ruby's room, no longer Arch's room. She sat next to Ruby, holding the older woman's free hand in hers. They sat silently until a nurse came to talk quietly to them, explaining.

Liz noticed little things while they waited; the dust particles in the streams of light from the sun; voices of two nurses down the hallway; how the room now seemed apart from the world, left out of real time, frozen instead in one solitary moment.

Finally Ruby stood, laying Arch's hand down gently on the blanket and smoothing his thin white hair to the side of his face. She leaned over, kissed him, and walked out the door.

Liz's throat tightened. She was having a hard time seeing through her tears. Touching the hospital blanket with her shaking fingers, she noticed the veins on his hands—intricate, complicated, finished.

"I love you, Arch," she spoke in a whisper. "I don't need to tell you how dearly Ruby loved you. She once told me I should grab hold of life. Go for the ride. My God, did the two of you ever do that."

She brushed his hand lovingly with hers. "You simply made up your mind to love, and then you loved, didn't you?"

Liz leaned forward to kiss his forehead, then left the room. She found Ruby standing near the picture window in the hospital lobby. She had been dressed for her granddaughter's wedding when Arch was stricken. Now she wanted to go to the reception.

It didn't occur to Liz to question Ruby. She simply led her out to her car and opened the passenger door for her. They entered the church hall and walked to Roger and Annie's side.

"He died. Just a little while ago," Ruby said brokenly. Jay came up to them and put a solid arm around Liz's waist. Ruby fought for a steady voice. "But you are celebrating a wonderful day. Arch and I had a good life together. I'll mourn him with all of you. Right now I could use a hug."

Liz watched Ruby move with Roger and Annie from family member to family member, repeating her news, comforting them even as they comforted her. Then she gathered coats and her daughters while Jay found Ben in the phone booth hiding from two of Annie's nieces.

He followed their car to the Red Door where Liz slowly walked up the steps and went into the house. The kids followed, quieter than usual.

Jay stepped into Liz's bathroom and turned on her shower, shutting the door to hold in the warmth. "Can I help you with your dress?" he asked.

"Please." He undid the long row of buttons and turning her around, kissed her tenderly. Then he left, shutting her bedroom door behind him.

The rest of the evening he played cards with the girls and oversaw Ben while he made popcorn. He carried Tess to bed after she fell asleep on the floor and suggested the same destination to Ben and Jane who went up without a fuss.

Cleaning up in the living room and kitchen, Jay finally went to Liz's door and knocking quietly, entered. His eyes adjusted to the dim light from the bathroom door left ajar. She was asleep, he thought, until he sat on the edge of her bed and saw her open eyes, staring like a wounded animal.

"Are you hungry?" he asked.

"What time is it?" she asked softly.

Jay peered at the clock beside her bed. "It's eight."

Liz sat up and swung her legs over the side of the bed, pushing her sweatshirt sleeves up. "The kids?"

He stood up as he answered. "They just went up to bed. Look, I just wanted to check on you before I left. I'll see you at church in the morning."

Liz held out a hand, stopping him before he could round the corner of her bed. "Would you mind staying for a little while? I can't...I just can't imagine Ruby's pain tonight. I'm having enough trouble with mine," she admitted with a brittle laugh.

Jay stacked logs and lit a fire while Liz put a tape in the player. They listened to music and visited long into the night.

The sound of dishes and pans clattering on the kitchen counter signaled morning. Ben was making breakfast. "Hey, Ben, what time is it?" Jay called out.

"About eight. We overslept, Mom. Isn't church at 8:30 this Sunday?"

She tumbled off the sofa and ran for her bedroom. Jay walked outside, still in his tuxedo, to check the morning's weather. He stuck his head back in the house long enough to tell Ben he'd meet them at church, then drove home to shower and change.

Liz and her children slipped into the pew in front of Jay a few minutes after the opening prayer. Father Bob gave a powerful sermon. A marriage, a death, and the beautiful sun-rise—metaphor fed metaphor and helped the readings come alive.

ନ୍ତର

Snow crystals sparkled, dancing in the air on Arch's funeral day making Liz glad she had taken her children to the wake the evening be-fore. They were in school today where it was warm.

The Morrison family took up the front third of the church. The rest was overflowing with friends, neighbors, and business acquaintances from Benton and surrounding communities. The respect and admiration felt for Arch was evident.

To do anything other than honor the life of Arch, Father Bob said, was to doubt there was any purpose to his time on earth. To feel hopelessness at his death was a sign we didn't believe in celebrating the end of this stage of life and the beginning of the next.

A son spoke briefly on behalf of the five children and Annie spoke for the grandchildren and great-grandchildren. Music filled the church throughout the service. One line about being raised up on eagle's wings stayed with Liz.

The grave side service was short, a concession to the frigid weather. Now came the second half of the celebration, the one where the official church role diminished and the role of friends and neighbors broadened.

Most of the people attending the burial returned to the church hall and shed their coats, taking the offered cups of coffee. Father Bob lead everyone in prayer.

Plates were heaped from a variety of dishes brought by parish members to comfort the family and mourn the passing of one of their own. Ruby and Liz found themselves next to one another in the dinner line. "Thanks for staying with me, Liz. It was a comfort."

Liz's eyes filled with tears as she dug futilely in her blazer and skirt pockets for a tissue. Jay, standing a few feet away, brought a handkerchief and a comment for her alone. Then he returned to where he'd been standing with Kent.

Liz dabbed her eyes, smiling weakly at Ruby. "Do you mind if I ask something about you and Arch?"

"Of course not."

"How do you love someone that much and not fear the future?" Liz asked, lowering her voice self-consciously. After the cold wind of the cemetery, she was finally getting warm.

"You're so busy living you don't give it one thought. Oh, we talked about the future but we didn't live in the future. Or the past for that matter. Just today. It's the only day you've got. And in case you think we had a fairy tale story, forget it."

Ruby looked at the people standing near her. They were all engrossed in their conversations. After dishing up a sampling of salads, she moved on down the table of food and whispered to Liz.

"We fought like everyone does, had rough spots in the road. We went through a number of financially difficult times and had trouble with children once in a while. But we'd decided from the very beginning that we wanted it to work and we never gave up."

They were in front of the dessert table. "The store's going to be closed the next two weeks, Liz. With Christmas and all, I think everyone will be busy enough, don't you?"

ဆာဌ

Christmas was in three days. Liz and the kids went out into the Robbins pasture to cut their own tree. Jay had told them they could have their pick, but hadn't offered to come help. Whatever the reason, she decided, the time apart was what she needed.

Ben proved to be good with the saw. With a rope they drug the tree the half mile back to the Red Door. The children holding onto it and tugging it through the snow and over the hills. They sang Christmas songs at the top of their voices and laughed at silly jokes Jane had learned from Fran that week.

While the girls moved baskets of magazines and wayward shoes to the side, Liz and Ben put the pine in the tree stand. Then they all admired their first tree in Benton, misshapen though it was. Their first in this wonderful old home, Liz told herself.

Christmas Eve they opened presents and snacked, enjoying the snowfall and the sound of Christmas music from their new CD player, a gift from Jay to their family. They dressed in their Christmas best and went to town for midnight Mass.

Liz had known Jay was going to spend this day in Kearney with his sister's family; he'd told her when he'd brought the gift by earlier in the week. She knew, too, that he was stepping back from her and she felt odd when he said nothing about it.

Christmas morning she and the children drove to Kearney and flew to New York, joining her sister Teresa and husband Dave and their two children in their Ithaca home for a few days. The kids were excited to see their cousins and grandparents. Anita and Raymond, Liz's other sister Megan and husband Paul and their children had also flown in.

When her mom asked about Jay, Liz's answer was short. The second time someone asked about him and received stony silence for an answer, Megan nudged Teresa and together they took Liz on an errand.

In a supermarket aisle, Teresa asked Liz about Jay, the man she'd heard about from their mother but not from Liz.

"He wants to have some kind of future with me. I don't know if I want one," Liz responded crossly, upset at having to discuss her private affairs.

"You don't want a future?" Megan asked sweetly. "Or not one with him?" Liz swallowed a sharp reply. After all, it would be foolish to argue with only a few days together.

Besides, she had to admit once she got back to Benton, the question had been a pretty good one. Liz's contract work picked up. She was busy every day with projects from The Source or at the Dirt Store.

Annie returned from her honeymoon. When they saw each other, she refrained from asking "the question" as Liz had come to think of it.

A few weeks passed. One day Annie walked into the store during Liz's lunch break and flopped down in an old chair.

"What's Jay up to?"

"I don't know," Liz mumbled between bites. She knew Annie's eyes were on her. At the sound of fingernails tapping on an armrest, Liz looked over. She admitted she hadn't seen much of him. "Not since before Christmas," Liz said, her face crumbling.

Annie's look softened. "Oh, Lizzy." She tugged on her arm gently. "I heard that he's been working in Kearney a lot. I guess his project is going well but he's very busy with it. Maybe he's just making up for lost time during the holidays."

"No," Liz said in a quiet but firm voice. "I screwed up. You warned me. My sisters even commented on my lack of, oh...vision for my future. I'd been wallowing in my own brand of self pity and I blew it." Liz stood up and dumped the rest of her coffee down the sink.

"Well, if you figured that out," Annie said, following her to the sink, "how hard could it be to..."

"Annie. I made light of his interest. Or at least I wasn't very responsive. You saw his school paper. He's not a light kind of guy. Just because he can laugh at life and find the fun doesn't mean he hasn't a brain or a feeling. And I knew that!" She said it forcefully, then more softly, "I knew that, and I still acted as if people like Jay come along every day. They don't. I realize that now."

"Fine." Annie pulled Liz's arm until she faced her. "So what are you going to do about it? Let him bow out or ask him to dance?"

"Ideally? Like in the movies?" Liz asked. "Why I'd go up to his house, knock on the door, and ask him to go out to dinner and talk his head off. Real world? Where you and I live? What should I do?"

Liz absently brushed some crumbs off her jeans. "I know it's my move," she nodded. "I frosted him with my stupid attitude. I have no problem swallowing my pride. That part isn't the problem."

"So what is?" Annie slid in fast, impatient for the point.

"What if I have to take rejection? I'm not sure I could handle it a second time."

℘℘

"Heard you were at the meeting at the fire hall last night," Bonnie commented between bites. She and Liz had met for a quick lunch at the Mustang.

Liz swallowed a drink of soda and nodded. She looked at her watch and glanced up at Bonnie. "Annie told me there was a meeting I should go to, that it might affect where the kids and I live, so I stepped in for a while. I was a little late getting there and I had some stuff to do at home so I didn't stay 'til the end."

"Long enough to catch what was going on?" Bonnie asked. She was in a hurry today, too. Both were hurriedly eating sandwiches and watching the time.

Liz nodded again. "I think so."

"And?" Bonnie asked. At the sound of the café door opening, she looked behind Liz and waved the newcomer over. Liz took another sip of her drink. She jumped when she heard Jay's voice greet them. Bonnie pushed a chair back for him to join them and he sat.

· After asking how Kent was doing, he looked over at Liz. "Saw you there last night," he commented.

Liz finished her last bite of sandwich and checked the time again. "I was just telling Bonnie that Annie had mentioned the meeting to me. I thought I should stop by and see for myself. That man, Gordie? Wasn't he the guy you talked with the day you picked me up out on Old Oak Road with the flat on my bike?"

The waitress came to take his order but he said he was waiting for someone. Turning back to Liz, he said it was. "So what did you learn?" he asked.

"Well," she said, wiping her mouth with a napkin and reaching in her jeans pocket for some cash, "I learned you've got county zoning but still a lot is left up to the county board members and they're not too anxious to say no to a businessman who lives among them."

She reached for the ticket, thanking Bonnie for inviting her. As Liz stood she looked back at Jay. "And Gordie isn't too worried about anyone else but himself. He wants to put in a huge cattle feeding operation and he doesn't really care if his neighbors are happy with that or not. Sounds like, from the size of the feedlot, that his neighbors are going to be people who live miles away from it, too."

Liz leaned on the back of her chair and low-ered her voice. "If I were you, Jay, I'd make a big stink. I have learned about the extreme polite-ness of neighbor toward neighbor when it comes to business in the rural countryside. I get that. But there's still the good of the community ver-sus the good of the individual and I say the com-munity has got to win every time. My advice, and it's free: go to the public hearing armed with facts, take people with you, and ask them to vote their consciences. And pressure the board like crazy."

She looked once more at her watch and then at Bonnie. "Gotta go, see you soon." She touched Jay's shoulder. "For what it's worth I think you did a great job leading the discussion. Pretty good job of keeping your cool, too. Well, all but that one time." She raised an eyebrow.

Behind her someone had entered the Mus-tang, and all three looked at the door. "She was at the meeting last night, too, wasn't she?" Liz asked Jay.

An attractive young blonde dressed in a pants suit looked around, then smiled and moved forward. She came to stand beside their table. "Sorry I'm late, Jay. Have you ordered for us?"

Jay made the introductions. "Karla, this is Liz Daniels. And this is my sister-in-law Bonnie Robbins. Karla Matthews." Liz excused herself after greeting Karla. She paid for the two lunches and stepped out into the overcast day.

She'd already turned on her ignition when there was a tap on her window. It was Bonnie. As it glided down, Liz apologized to her for their hurried lunch. "I've got a project I wanted to get finished today and I needed a couple hours before the kids got home from school to do it."

"No problem. Thanks for paying. Any idea who Karla is?"

Liz looked at the Mustang's front door. "I don't know," she said, shaking her head. "I'd heard Jay was seen with a gorgeous young blonde lately. I'd say that would be her."

Bonnie frowned at Liz, then looked back at the café. "He hasn't said a word to me. Hmm, I wonder what he's up to?"

Liz's laugh was hollow.

"No," Bonnie said, "I mean, I wonder what they're working on. Oh, if you think he and she... No, I don't think so."

This time it was Bonnie who laughed. Then backing away from the Toyota, she waved to Liz and walked to her Suburban across the street.

Looking back, Liz realized later, there had been no indication her life was about to change. That evening she cooked Chinese food for her children and a couple of their friends. They made popcorn and everyone watched a movie, some adventure thing or another. She didn't pay much attention to it.

Her mind was on Jay's absence the past few weeks. After the movie ended, she took Ben and Jane's friends home.

&⊃⊂&

At exactly eleven-thirty Liz walked out of St. Mary's Church and stood visiting with friends on the front lawn.

"Did you hear the big news out of Lincoln?" Jay had stopped by to say hello when John came up to them with the news. "The governor just announced some big bucks to pull together the various economic development and advocacy groups and get them working on some pretty major projects. I mean big bucks. And he's putting it all in Lincoln, where everything else is, surrounded by officialdom."

Liz noticed Jay bristle and how agitated John was as he talked. John's wife Jennifer nodded in disgust. The chilly winter air soon ended their talk and everyone left for home.

Liz finished reading the newspaper article John had mentioned that morning as she munched on strips of meat and cheese meant for a tossed salad. She could see why Jay and John were upset. The proposal had the distinct odor of a doomed project.

As she so often did these days when she wanted to think something through, she pulled on her hiking boots, grabbed her coat, and told Jane where she was going. Outside in the cold, wind snapping at her clothes, she began climbing the hill beyond the barn. There was no way around it; January was ugly in Benton. The colors were variations of the same drab brown and gray.

The saving grace was that she had seen summer and fall. Was it just her fantasy or was winter masking a beautiful season around the corner. She fervently hoped so, and shivering, trudged on.

What was that Jay had said to John after church? "Yeah, I saw the story." Resignation sliced into each word. "Our way of life, the rural way of life, is dying. Oh sure, it's been changing since the fifties. Actually since the rise of the Industrial Revolution. We've had fallout in agriculture ever since the agrarian culture began to decline. But ranches and farms everywhere are having a hell of a time making it now. Kent and Bonnie are struggling like crazy to just hold on. So are Frank Mundi and Steve Johnson and nearly everyone else, bar the biggest operations, and even they're learning what it means to worry about paying bank loans and surviving."

John had nodded, silently agreeing. Jay had spoken again. "The bureaucrats say this is just a cycle. The board of trade boys and Ag credit people and even the secretary of agriculture say the same thing. But it's bigger than that."

Jay had kicked a car tire, then frowned in the direction of his listeners. "It's nice to know the governor is aware of how bad things are out here. Good to see him dedicating resources. It's more than I expected, frankly. But this plan of his isn't going to make a damn dent. I hate to see the money and time, let alone the promise of something good, fail because they didn't get the right kind of input in the first place."

Liz had listened carefully. She was learning just how deep a love for his ranch he had. "Me," Jay had added, "I'm immune to this for the most part. I can do projects anywhere. I'm relatively safe, my income is pretty secure. I'm one of the lucky ones."

He had vented again, this time kicking a lifeless weed from between the cracks at the curb, its' winter roots giving way to his lackluster temper. "A lot of people here don't have those options. Kent cuts back every year. He drives old pickups, holds equipment together with a welder and baling twine, constantly puts off making capital purchases he sorely needs to make because there just isn't any money."

"Why in the hell," he had suddenly thundered, "when the people in a position to help...why the hell don't they ask us what we need? Ask for our ideas? My God, we're not idiots! Why don't they build a complete, comprehensive plan and have everyone come to the table to give it some go?"

He had spoken quietly—disgust and, worse yet, resignation—in every word. "And why do they give up on farms and ranches? Nothing in the article mentions any help to them, only to the towns. They've still got a sink-or-swim philosophy about agriculture. Just want to help out the middle-sized towns and maybe that will help the smaller towns. And so on. Band-Aids. That's all they're really handing out. Who exactly do they think is going to start healing the whole cycle when the farmer and rancher can't buy a single damn thing from the guy in town? Can't—no matter how hard they work—pay their bills?"

It would be futile. She knew that. Getting in to see the governor would be impossible. And even then, who would she say she represented?

The Robbins family? What would she use for credibility? It was useless to think about it. There was nothing she could do. And that would have been the end of it.

After school on Wednesday she got a call from Father Bob asking if she could substitute that evening for the ninth grade religious education teacher. She agreed and went a little early to look over the material.

Her class was small, only a dozen kids who were, for the most part, well-behaved. The subject that evening was on being a leader, a disciple. The discussion was halting, interspersed with snickers and wisecracks. Working on developing a faith life—particularly in front of your peers—was painful at this age.

Then one of the boys turned her question back on her. "How about you? What do you think it means to be a leader?"

"Well," Liz said slowly, forming her thoughts as she spoke, "I suppose doing what I think is right, whether or not it's popular or smooth. Even if it makes me stand out in front of people in a way that makes me uncomfortable. Even if it's not successful and I know ahead of time it's not going to be."

The class ended with a couple of work sheets. When class was finished, she gathered her children and drove home. Sitting in front of the fireplace after the kids were in bed, she watched the logs go ruddy red. The flames receded, their snapping slowly drowned out by her thoughts.

Annie dropped by after speech practice to borrow a jacket and stayed to enjoy a cup of hot chocolate with Liz. "How'd class go tonight?" she asked.

"Fine. Wonderful," Liz responded woodenly.

"You sound enthused," Annie said. She looked closely at Liz. "Have some trouble?"

"A lot," Liz answered, sighing.

"The Broad kid acting up again?" Annie was ready to commiserate or to offer some hints on classroom management to her friend.

But Liz shook her head, still staring at the fire. "No, the kids were fine. We had a good discussion tonight. The trouble is with me."

She snuggled her feet up under her and burrowed into the back of the sofa, shifting until she was comfortable. "I can't get something out of my mind, something I heard after church last weekend. About the development plan the governor hopes to instigate."

"I read that," Annie nodded. She waited for Liz to go on.

"Well, I can't forget it," Liz began. "In my line of work it takes a huge amount of effort to see a project through. Just tremendous work ethic, and determination. You'll succeed if you work hard and have a strong, focused plan when you begin."

She leaned her head back and stared at the ceiling. "Jay's right. The powers that be didn't think this plan through, didn't consult with enough of the right people. And someone needs to get involved instead of just saying 'oh well, darn it, this won't be nearly as good as it could be but I guess it's better than nothing.' I guess I need to do this for me."

⟡

"Good morning...Governor Moreland's office." "Good morning...Lt. Governor Baldwin's office." "Good morning..." "Good morning..." "Good morning..." "Good morning..." "Good morning...Chief of Staff Behlend's office."

"Good morning, this is Liz Daniels. I'd like to speak with Mr. Behlend." She was into her second hour of trying to reach out and touch anyone.

"Just one moment, please." Strumming her fingers on the table beside her computer, she studied the web page in front of her. The governor's staff was listed as were the various state agencies.

She'd worked her way through much of the top end and had gotten as far as the office administrative assistant, maybe, in each case.

"Hello, Angie Soukup, Mr. Behlend's assistant. May I help you?"

"Hello, Ms. Soukup. This is Liz Daniels calling from Benton, Nebraska."

"Good morning. What can I do for you? And it's Angie."

"Angie, please call me Liz. I'd like to speak with Mr. Behlend. I've been reading up on his involvements prior to going to work for Governor Moreland. I think he may be just the person I need to talk with concerning the governor's plan to enhance economic development work in the state."

"I'm sorry, who did you say you were with?"

Here goes, she thought. "I'm a consultant with The Source, a public relations firm out of Minneapolis. I work with about a dozen large, established clients on image and media outreach projects."

"And what do you want with the chief of staff?"

"I'd like fifteen minutes of his time, anywhere he wants to meet, to discuss a proposal I have for him. I represent no group, no agenda. And I would very much appreciate it if you'd say yes, you'll schedule me in."

She'll say no, of course, Liz thought, but she would just keep working the flow chart of authority until she talked face-to-face with someone, or until she aged another year, whichever came first.

"Exactly what do you want to talk about?" Accustomed to caution, Angie's voice communicated nothing.

"That's what I want the fifteen for, Angie. But the reason I'm calling is," she swallowed quickly. "I moved from Minneapolis to Benton a year ago. I work in the public relations field and consult primarily with corporations and political campaigns. I've dealt with the Minneapolis and national media extensively."

She pushed back from the screen and concentrated. "I now live in the country near a little community where agriculture is the major industry. I believe that the governor's plan is leaving some important components out. I'm not very informed on agriculture, but PR I know."

She chewed on her lower lip, hoping she was emitting more confidence than she felt.

"If the governor truly wants this proposal of his to work, and if he wants to look like a winner during this election year, then I strongly urge you to help me meet with Mr. Behlend to talk. That's it, just talk. He doesn't have to agree to a thing if he'll simply give me a few minutes of his time."

Seconds ticking on the clock, Liz reached for her coffee. Then Angie spoke. "He couldn't agree to anything, Liz. He doesn't have that kind of authority."

Liz smiled slowly, setting her cup down again. "Of course not, Angie. I understand. All I'm saying is I'd like to visit, no strings attached, and see what he thinks."

Come on Angie, Liz coaxed, be curious enough to take a risk. "I didn't call the governor's opponent because I was hopeful I could visit with your camp first and be of some service." She just mentioned it, and then dropped it.

Angie decided. "Tomorrow morning. Could you come to my office at the Capitol tomorrow at ten o'clock? After that we're going on a trade trip to Brazil and won't be back for five days."

Liz closed her eyes. Tomorrow. "Thank you. I'll see you at ten."

Force of habit led her to pack an overnight bag with clothes for Saturday just in case. Corporate trips had taught her that being prepared was more than a motto.

She spent extra time with her kids that evening and went to bed early, determined to be well rested for her trip. She would wake Ben and the girls before she left. They would have to get their own cereal breakfast and be ready for the bus.

The drive took a little more than three hours. By the time she arrived in Lincoln she was anxious for her meeting. The governor's mansion and the Capitol came into view quickly, thanks to Annie's map. Glancing at her watch she knew she had time to freshen up, relax a little, maybe even play tourist.

She was studying the intricately carved doors on the entrance to the legislative chambers when a lean, graying man stepped hurriedly out of the chambers and accidentally bumped her to the side.

Turning to apologize, he offered to help her find the individual she was looking for inside.

"Actually," Liz countered, "I'm meeting Mr. Behlend's assistant Angie Soukup in a little while and I was just taking a self-guided tour."

"Would you like me to show you to the chief of staff's office?" he offered.

"I would, thank you." She held out her hand, "I'm Liz Daniels."

"How do you do, I'm Vic Moreland."

Liz collected herself quickly. "I apologize for not recognizing you, Governor. I've only lived in Nebraska a short time and I didn't recognize you from newspaper photos."

"Not too flattering, are they?" he allowed, none too amused. They walked down the administrative wing and into the doorway of his office to show Liz where it was located, then to the next door.

"I'll just tell Angie you're here."

"Thank you, Governor, I appreciate that." She stepped forward. "Governor Moreland, I'd like a few minutes of your time this morning, as well. Would that be possible?"

"I'm afraid it isn't, Ms. Daniels. I'm leaving Tuesday for a junket to Brazil, a trade mission actually, and I'm trying to tie up loose ends today. I'm booked solid. Nice meeting you." They shook hands and he walked out the north door.

She moved around the office, studying photos on the wall and noting inscriptions on the plaques. "To Jim Behlend, friend of development efforts everywhere." "Jim Behlend, agriculture supporter." "Our man in government. Small Town. USA."

The door behind her opened and she turned to see a woman in her forties enter the door the governor had just exited, gliding forward in a wheelchair.

"I hear Governor Moreland showed you here. Nice going, Liz. I'm Angie." They shook hands, both grasping firmly, taking one another's measure. "Would you like some coffee? Tea?"

"No thank you. I intend to put my fifteen minutes to good use."

Angie moved closer, ready to listen.

Liz knew it was the opening comment that would make or break her. "I've pulled up the past ten years of news items which mention Mr. Behlend's name."

"What did your research tell you?" Angie quizzed her politely.

"That his name shows up in places kind of surprising for a Republican in a Republican state. If I didn't know better I'd think he was a latent Democrat."

Behlend's assistant laughed out loud. Liz smiled and continued "Or is the better phrase a liberal conservative, or maybe a conservative liberal?"

"What do you think?" Angie replied.

She was good. Deflecting it, Angie was waiting to see how the land lay. Liz answered. "Oh, I don't know, maybe all of the above. And I really don't care about politics, Angie." She got a raised eyebrow out of that.

"I told you on the phone that I haven't got an agenda, political or otherwise. I just need to find someone in state government, someone with good access to the governor, who is open to ideas, who honestly supports rural areas and small towns, and who doesn't kowtow to big business interests over the needs and interests of the little guy. I'll keep his secret, Angie, but I want you to do something for me."

For now she just wanted Angie's attention. She'd work on her support after that. "I can help the governor quietly, behind the scenes, to reshape this plan of his so that it will succeed. I can help all of you pull together the best people to make it a better plan and at the same time keep you from losing face. No one will know how and where we tinkered with it, and in a couple weeks, still well before the primaries, I can help you and the media release this to the general public."

Liz shifted in her chair but kept her eyes focused on Angie. "Citizens will eat it up, the media will love it, agriculture will benefit, the advocacy and development groups will be able to roll their sleeves up and do what they do best; there are no losers."

They were interrupted by her secretary with a phone call and twice with a reminder of an appointment's arrival.

Each time, Angie turned them away, either toward Behlend or postponing until afternoon. Finally, after asking that the rest of her calls be held, Angie invited Liz to join her for an early lunch. It was shortly after eleven.

Liz declined, apologizing for keeping her so long. "But I sincerely appreciate the time you've given me this morning."

"You're welcome, Liz. And I think you should reconsider lunch."

What was she getting at?

"The chief of staff and I are going to visit in his office over lunch. We're having sandwiches brought in."

Liz was suddenly ravenous. She asked for directions to the nearest restroom, wanting to mentally compose herself for this opportunity. She'd wanted this meeting but had not counted on it.

Angie was waiting for Liz in the hallway and together they entered the office of Jim Behlend. He hung up his phone.

"Mr. Behlend, I'd like to introduce Liz Daniels whom I was just telling you about a minute ago. Liz, this is Jim Behlend." They shook hands.

"Angie says you've been having an interesting visit this morning, Ms. Daniels. She thought it should continue here. We've got a few details for our trip to go over first and then we can all talk."

While the two hashed out last minute instructions on their itinerary, Liz studied the shelves of books. Philosophy, history, political science, biographies; it seemed Jim Behlend had many consultants.

Five minutes later they invited Liz to join them at a small table in a corner of the office and lunch was brought in. They ate in silence for a few minutes. "Liz, tell me why you're here," Jim began.

She answered immediately. "Because I work in public relations. I've observed different governmental and corporate entities and how they work together in a variety of situations and I am pretty astute at sensing internal problems, problems which are difficult to recognize from inside because of the various hats the leaders wear."

She glanced across the table at Angie. "As I told Ms. Soukup, I'm not representing anyone specific so I'm not wearing a particular hat. I come with no prejudices or agendas. I just know that the plan as set forth by the Governor late last week won't work because some extremely important components of a successful plan are missing—consensus and participation among these."

She stood up and took her glass of water with her. Change the pace, move the setting slightly, show your authority; work it, she told herself.

"I am by no means a planning specialist in government programs. But," she smiled at them, "that is my point. This shouldn't be operated like other agency programs. The office shouldn't be in Lincoln. The programs and planning should be far more accessible to those you're trying to reach. And it should be far more flexible than outlined in the media stories. What else?"

She knew she was blowing her budget. She also knew that now was the time to do it. "You need to quietly, privately meet with a list of people I can provide for more in-depth planning so that you don't miss any bases."

Setting her glass down, she chose a book on the settling of Nebraska from a shelf and held it, completely at ease. Time to set the bait. "I can get you contacts from around the state in a few days time. They'll form a short-lived advisory team to help realign your plan. I'll assist you in how you work this so that it will get the most exposure possible when you're finished."

"We'll bring in the development people, some reputable rural representatives, highly respected advocacy groups, people who've put together very creative coalitions and partnerships, and ask them to work with us. And we'll do it so quietly, so fast, that in a few days, Governor Moreland will be able to walk up to the podium and announce that due to the seriousness of the agricultural situation in his state, he's stepped up his original plan and given it more authority, wider scope, and an advisory team that will knock the socks off everyone who reads and listens to the news coverage."

Liz was done. They could buy into this altruistically, politically, or psycho graphically.

Behlend blinked, looked at Angie, then back at Liz. "I'll give it some thought." He nodded to Liz, "Thanks for coming today."

Shaking her hand and nodding to his assistant, Behlend left the room. Angie, too, shook Liz's hand, thanked her for coming, and rolled forward to show her to the outer door.

Two minutes later Liz was on the street outside the State House. It looked as if they were interested enough to listen but not motivated enough to buy. On the other hand, until she heard no she wouldn't be certain whether she had succeeded or failed.

Liz drove to Centennial Mall, also on Annie's map, and found a gift store featuring Nebraska products. She purchased a number of items from across the state and called a courier service from a listing she found in the yellow pages.

The saleswoman was helpful, offering Liz work space to assemble the two baskets and to write a note for each. When the courier arrived, she arranged for the delivery to Angie and Jim, paying to get the baskets there as soon as possible, and to deliver into their hands alone. Interrupt a meeting if necessary, she instructed him, but get the baskets there now.

Outside of stopping in Kearney to fuel up, she drove straight through and arrived home by five-thirty. The kids were home, already starting hamburgers. She unwound for a few minutes, visiting with her children, and before she knew it someone was touching her shoulder.

"Want to eat, Mom?" Ben asked.

"What time is it?" she asked, confused.

"It's eight. Tess went to bed about an hour ago and Jane just went up. I thought I'd wake you before I go to bed. You hungry?"

She stretched and shook her hair back from her eyes, staring at Ben.

"We saved your hamburger in some foil and put it in the oven on low. Jane told me you do that to keep them from getting too dry."

Liz ate while sitting at the counter, wondering if her day had been a waste of time. There she'd gone, flying off to Lincoln like a female knight on her shining stead, thinking she was going to save ruraldom and slay all the problems.

Okay, maybe she had gotten her foot in the door. Sure, they had listened to her. Actually, she grinned, that part had been pretty good.

She wiped a dab of ketchup off her lip and took her plate to the sink, rinsing it off and stacking it with the other plates in the dishwasher. But what had really happened? She'd been dismissed when lunch ended. On the other hand, maybe she had given them some things to think about, and she'd gotten pretty close to the governor's office, hadn't she?

That's probably the end of it, she decided. This thought was strangely dissatisfying. Before she had always followed through. But, she reminded herself, this wasn't her project. It was one she had wanted. How well she knew that power was in who had the control.

Annie's birthday was the next Friday and Liz was having a party for her. She served homemade pizzas and a huge tossed salad to a few of their mutual women friends. After strawberry cheesecake with a candle in the middle, they sat around visiting.

When the phone rang Annie went to answer it in the kitchen, then beckoned to Liz. "It's the governor's office," she said as she handed it to her.

"Right!" Liz answered, "and I'm Barbra Streisand." She took the receiver and stepped back into the kitchen where she could hear better. "This is Liz."

"Liz, this is Jim Behlend. How are you this evening?" She stared at Annie who was mouthing "I told you so."

"I'm doing well, Jim. We're having a birthday celebration so it's a little loud. What can I do for you?"

"I wondered if you could come to Lincoln on Monday and discuss your ideas with us." She gave one of Ben's silent cheers. Annie started grinning.

"Who will be at this meeting?"

"Well, Angie and I had some time to talk about your proposal during our trip to Brazil. We talked with the governor on our way home yesterday and the three of us would like to meet with you. Will Monday work?"

"I'll be in your office at eleven o'clock. How does that sound?"

"Let me check here." He was silent, studying his and the governor's calendars. "Yes, that will work for us. We'll see you Monday at eleven."

She replaced the phone in the base. "I don't believe it. They want a face to face. The governor, too."

Annie had a puzzled expression on her face. "Why would that surprise you? You're good at what you do." Annie put her arm around Liz's shoulder and together they rejoined the party.

"Hey! Guess what? Liz is having lunch with the governor Monday," Annie crowed.

"I'm not sure what we'll talk about," Liz said after explaining, "but I am really pleased to be getting my foot in the door. Actually," she said with a nervous chuckle, "I'm terrified I don't know enough about what I'm talking about and I'll screw the whole thing up."

Annie held up two fingers. "Twice," she said. "You got your foot in the door twice. That's something right there. Keep it up."

Shortly afterward the party broke up. Annie thanked Liz for the nice evening, asking if she would see her before she went to Lincoln.

"I'll try. And Annie? If something happens and I don't get home in good time, could the kids go home with you?"

"Absolutely. I'll plan on it unless I hear otherwise. See you." She hugged Liz and left.

12

L incoln was a different experience this time. She knew where she was going and what she was walking into. She was prepared.

It being an election year didn't hurt. Liz had worked enough events to understand the politics of these matters. But being in the inner office, discussing image issues and deal-making reminded her of all she disliked about PR, too.

Vic Moreland was an instinctive politician. And his advisors believed he was in trouble. He needed to make a score before the primary in order to stay in the governor's Mansion.

This rural initiative, as his aides were calling it, had to either make him big points or go quietly into the night. It could help him, but it had damn well better not hurt him.

Liz realized that it was merely a political move, this interest on his part. She also knew that was the tack she would take to reach him. Moreland, Angie, and Jim Behlend were already in the governor's office when she arrived.

Moreland was sharing the message from his church service yesterday, praising the visiting pastor's sermon. Liz did not see a particular bond between Behlend and the governor and this intrigued her.

If they were not buddies or allies, she concluded, then Behlend must be talented at attaching his interests to those of the governor. It seemed she had stumbled on the correct advocate.

"Now suppose we get down to business," Moreland said, his demeanor changed. "I've had your credentials checked, Ms. Daniels. It appears we have here," he looked at Behlend, "a bonafide public relations mavin. Your associates in Minneapolis speak highly of you. Very highly. They say you are to be trusted, in opinion and with conversations. So, Ms. Daniels, what are you offering me?"

"Governor, please call me Liz." She smiled and he nodded graciously. "I'm offering you the attention of the news media and the general public shortly before the primary election." She paused ever so briefly. "The backing of a reworked rural initiative under my guidance and all of our..." gesturing to the four of them "input." She stopped there. Offer any more and she'd have to prove each point.

"And exactly how are you proposing to do this?"

"Governor Moreland," she laughed confidently, "I thought you'd never ask." She walked over to her briefcase and opened it, carrying it with her as she returned to her chair. Arranging the briefcase on a side table and shuffling through the papers, she did her version of a Mary Sue Parker.

She let the others focus on her, wait for her. Liz was now in charge of the meeting. She found what she was looking for and passed a copy to Governor Moreland.

She then handed copies to Angie and Jim and began. Summarizing the assumptions and goals on the sheet, she led them through her plan to beef up the rural initiative by bringing in a list of advisors with irrefutable credibility. Advisors from across the state. Advisors who would fill out this plan, attract media attention, and gain the governor votes.

She wove the plan and the election together. And the governor liked it. He really liked it.

He could care less what the plan was or did. The initial development plan had been obviously concocted by others than himself. He'd gone along with it, fishing for 3rd District and rural 1st and 2nd District votes.

When its announcement had been received with a lukewarm response, he'd all but lost interest in it. But now the Daniels woman would do all the work and promised to hand him the attention of the voters, to boot. He liked how it sounded and he listened closely.

Jim asked a few questions and Angie took notes. The two were genuinely attentive. Liz finished her presentation in under twenty minutes. She stuffed papers back into her briefcase and stood.

Turning expectantly toward the governor, a pleasant smile on her lips, she asked him to show her to her work space. Moreland had already made up his mind. He smoothly walked to the door, opened it, and gestured for Liz to follow him.

Leading the way down the hallway, he entered a doorway to his right. "There's a desk, computer, three phone lines, heck! even a window with a view!" the governor chuckled as he gestured to Jim.

The two men left the room. Angie rolled around to face Liz and the two eyed one another. "I will remember what I've just seen here for a long time," Angie said solemnly. "And when I want something very badly, I will call you."

Liz exhaled. "Believe me, Angie, I'll take that call. Thanks to you I got both feet in the door." Walking over to the desk, she looked at the computer equipment. "Now, what kind of programs are loaded on this and how do I get in contact with support staff here, and tell me about the phone system, will you?"

After adjusting the lighting Liz got to work. Four hours later a phone call was directed to Liz's office. She picked up the handset and quietly answered. "Hello."

"Hello to you."

She dropped her pen.

"Jay. How did you find me?"

"I heard about a woman from Benton who was on a mission. Had a feeling it was you. By the way, exactly where are you?"

"I'm in my new temp office in the State House." There was silence for a few seconds.

"You did it." His voice was even, but she thought she detected an edge to it.

"I'm here for now."

"What are your plans?"

She sighed, the day already catching up with her. "I'm here for the duration. I don't know how long that will be, and I don't know exactly what I'll be doing even tomorrow. But I've got office space, all the support staff I need, and the governor's blessing."

Jay asked about her meeting with the governor. "I suppose this is what I was hoping would happen," he said when she was finished.

Liz moved a notebook aside and stared out the window. "What do you mean?" she asked softly.

He cleared his throat. "I'll be straight with you, Liz, I'm ticked you're there. I think I put this in your head and I've tried not to ask anything of you."

A dozen possible replies raced through her brain. She settled on the most direct one. "I'm just doing this because...I don't know, I suppose because I can. And I got lucky and found someone to listen to me." One of her phone lines started blinking. "I've got a call waiting."

"Just one thing."

She found her heartbeat picking up at the sensual resonance in his voice.

"I'm not really asking, I'm telling. What you're doing means a lot to everyone out here in the country. Call me if I can help."

"I will. I'm leaving soon to get a motel and put my feet up. And I think later I'm going to eat a whole Nebraska raised and fed steer I am so hungry."

He grinned as he turned off his cell and finished at the project site for the day.

She smiled and gathered her papers into her briefcase.

The next day Liz accomplished more than she thought was humanly possible. She called on the staff for faxing, dictation, and phone numbers throughout the morning. She made ten calls by noon and had curled up on the sofa—she'd had one brought in for casual conversations she planned to host later in the week—for half an hour while phoning three western Nebraska Ag leaders.

Jim Behlend was in twice to offer his help and lend some ideas. Angie came in nearly every hour and left each time with two or three jobs. The governor called her a little after twelve, inviting her to his office for lunch. She entered and found they would be dining alone.

He gallantly pulled back her chair, setting his close to her. Liz made a point of asking him questions about his political career and his business interests before he'd entered politics. Since he enjoyed talking about himself, the lunch time ended quickly, Moreland not yet exhausting the subject.

Liz excused herself and returned to her office, meeting Jim along the way. He turned and followed her in the door. Liz settled herself at her desk and Behlend pulled up a chair. "Looks like you're hard at it. How's it going?"

Liz handed him two pages she'd printed out before lunch. On it were lists of phone calls, faxed papers, people contacted and their associations with groups, businesses, or political entities.

She also had documented every meeting with Angie, Jim, the governor, and support staff members and indicated the purpose and outcome of each meeting. Her comments from her calls were noted at the end of each line. Basically this was an accounting of her time and work plan, piece by piece, and in order of occurrence.

Behlend's smile as he handed the papers back to her was huge. "That's the most complete report I believe I've ever seen on a project, particularly one begun only yesterday and still in its infancy."

She shook her head. "This project is four or five years old already, Jim. It has to be. This baby is growing fast and I have to stay ahead of it." She reached for another sheet and handed it to him.

"I need several contacts made. I wonder if you could make them for me? Also, I need about three people, good on the phone, to meet with me in an hour and I'll use them the rest of the afternoon and probably tomorrow. Can you do that?"

That evening before she left for her motel she called Annie and Roger's. Tess answered. Now a six-year-old, she rushed for the phone every time it rang.

"Mom! I knew it was you. I miss you." Annie pulled her up onto her lap, letting Tess talk and motioning to the rest to gather around for their turn with their mom.

Liz chatted with all of them about school, homework, and the latest story about their friends before asking for Annie. She came on the line.

"They're thrilled you called," she told Liz.

"How is everything?" Liz asked, needing to feel connected, like she was at home instead of alone in Lincoln.

"Really good. The kids are doing fine. Roger's having a ball with them. He's told me twice you'll have to fight him to get them back."

Liz grinned at this.

Wednesday was impossible. People were unresponsive. Moving them to commitments was nearly undoable. But the undoable deal had been Liz's forte in Minneapolis.

She was pushing. Four office staff were now dedicated to her and were working out of another temporary office two doors down from hers.

Calling in debts to Moreland and creating new ones, she conferred often with Behlend and the governor on who owed what to whom.

"Mr. Salak. This is Liz Daniels calling from Governor Moreland's office." She listened to his greeting. "The governor is working on his rural development initiative and we're asking for your support in southwest Nebraska...I understand. I'm sorry to hear you feel that way...Yes, I realize that your part of the state has not necessarily been flooded with assistance recently."

She glanced out the window, wishing for her view from home. The sight of wind-swirled fallen leaves outside made her long for a fast hike in the pastures above her house. The gray world surrounding the Capitol was little different from the gray at home. Except she wasn't home.

Liz finished her call, receiving a half-hearted yes. She worked through the lunch time and well into the afternoon. She called Roger and Annie's after the kids arrived from school and talked with them, soaking in their young and excited voices.

Behlend was walking down the hallway late the next afternoon when he saw a man coming toward him, obviously looking for someone. Jim stopped and introduced himself.

"Jay Robbins. Nice to meet you, Jim. I'm looking for Liz Daniels. Can you show me her work space?"

"Sure. Follow me."

They walked into Liz's office. When Jay followed Behlend in, she paused, her eyes widening, then continued talking into the phone, motioning them to the sofa. Jim stepped back into the hallway to speak to someone, then came back in the room and struck up a conversation with Jay.

"There is no way that I can accept that answer Mr. Garner," Liz was saying. She listened to the voice on the other end of the line and ignored her audience of two. "Whether or not you like it, this rural initiative now does have teeth in it and I'm afraid you will have to do your job. I'm sorry if this will make more work for you, I truly am. But please explain the point of working for rural economic development if you're not really working for it."

She listened to his long reply and began to smile. "That is kind of you. I will be sure to pass on your regards to the governor. So I can count on you to attend the press conference? Wonderful. I look forward to meeting you at the reception afterwards. Goodbye, Mr. Garner."

"I've got to catch someone," she spared a quick look at Jay. "I'll be right back," and hurriedly left the room.

Jay looked at Behlend. "Pretty determined, isn't she?" he commented.

"She's the most competent consultant I believe I've ever witnessed," Jim agreed.

The phone rang and he went to answer it. While he was talking, Liz walked back in and went over to the sofa, sitting down with a tired sigh. "What are you doing in Lincoln?" she asked.

Jay told her about a client from Albuquerque who had called wanting him to look at a site in Lincoln for a new restaurant.

Jim hung up the phone and drew up a chair and the three visited about Jay's work and what Liz had accomplished thus far.

Behlend noticed the regard Jay paid Liz and how tired she looked. "I have a suggestion for you, Liz," he said as he stood. "Go to your motel and take it easy. And don't get here too early tomorrow morning. We want to have this big media event you keep promising us and we want you there, not sick from exhaustion."

She walked over to her desk, glanced at her watch, and after a brief internal struggle, shut down her computer. She'd done enough for one day. Jim and Jay walked with her down the hallway and into the chief of staff's office to tell Angie they were leaving, then next door to bid the governor a good evening.

Introducing Jay to Vic Moreland, Liz commented that his family was one of the reasons she was working the phones and confiscating state employees. The governor shook Jay's hand. "She appears to be getting the job done. Pretty good PR person, isn't she?"

Jay shot Moreland a steady look. "No, Governor, she's a very good PR person. You're lucky to have her," he said, looking at Liz. She cleared her throat and walked to the door.

The three moved outside to the front of the State House. Coming to the end of the sidewalk, Behlend asked Jay about the restaurant site.

Liz suddenly was very tired and Jay, sensing this, broke off his answer to Jim and taking Liz's arm walked her to her vehicle. He followed her with his pickup to her motel where they had supper in the motel restaurant.

"Are you sure you wouldn't rather go out and eat?" she asked. "How often do you end up in a town with all this choice?" She was grateful, though, for the quiet night. After ordering off the menu, Liz settled back and eased her aching muscles. "I'm surprised to see you here, Jay. Really surprised."

He set down his drink and picked up her hand, his eyes steady on hers. They were seated in a small booth in the back of the spacious restaurant.

"You shouldn't be. I think I've made it pretty plain how I feel."

Maybe it was the different setting. Or the four days of power working in an environment in which she was very comfortable. Whatever the reason, Liz gave voice to what she'd wondered, even agonized over for weeks.

"I thought you were playing the field," she said calmly, studying his face. "I'd heard about Karla even before you introduced me to her. And I haven't seen you around lately, so I guess I'm surprised to see you here now."

"Karla. Yes." Jay's eyes were gleaming as he reached for his billfold and drew out a business card, handing it to Liz. "Jealous? Because if you are I'd say we've made major headway in this thing that we aren't calling a relationship."

His cool look annoyed her. She took the card and read Karla's name. And her title. And that she was with the State of Nebraska as a consultant to counties on zoning issues. "I think she's gorgeous," Liz commented softly, handing back the card.

"Yeah," he agreed, cheerfully nodding. "She's a fine looking woman. Got a great head on her shoulders. Is doing a heck of a job. I seem to have a talent for locating women like that."

She glanced up at him.

"It's you I'm interested in. I thought you wanted some time to think about us and I've got to tell you, it was no easy task giving it to you."

Her eyes flickered, then locked with his. "Okay," she said at last.

Jay thanked the waiter when he brought their salads and a basket of bread.

Then Liz told him about the huge day she had planned for tomorrow and probably part of Saturday. She hoped to make it home for part of the weekend.

"I've got to be back here Monday morning first thing and then Tuesday is the news conference. We're going to spend most of Monday lining that up and finishing up our calls around the state. We meet with our new advisory group Monday night at the governor's Mansion."

Liz reached for her fork. "You're welcome to come to the reception we're having Tuesday. The press conference will be at ten and the reception about ten-thirty." She waited for his nod. "So what are your ideas for this restaurant?"

She slept 'til after eight and took a leisurely shower. By the time she arrived at her office at nine-thirty, the executive wing was wondering where she was.

Jay had told her he had an early meeting with the current owner of the potential site and then was leaving for home. He was going to be in Albuquerque early next week, meeting with the restaurant owner and wasn't sure he could get back for the reception Tuesday.

Liz now stepped into high gear. She called in her temporary staff and assigned multiple jobs, then set about making more phone calls. Things were moving ahead of schedule and she could afford to add to her plan.

She put in a call to Minneapolis after visiting briefly with Behlend and the governor. "I want to bring in a couple more PR people to help me," she had told them. "I suppose anyone could do what I want them to do, but I want the best; people I've worked with before who know how to do it right and what not to do."

Her visit with Kevin at The Source went well. Pete and Sandra would be on the first flight Monday morning and stay through Tuesday afternoon. She intended to burn some midnight oil while they were here and be ready for the press conference and follow-up meeting with the advisory group.

℘℃Ↄ℞

Kent and Jay were eating at Lots. Neither had felt like a home cooked hamburger or a can of soup, their basic repertoire when they were the cooks. "So how's it going for her down there? Is she getting Lincolnitis yet?" Kent asked.

He was amused with Jay. After years of being told to take it easy, quit worrying, see the big picture, he could finally give a little of his brother's razzing back.

"No, I don't think so," Jay answered. "It must be a pleasure to walk out your office door and have half a dozen good restaurants within a few minutes. I don't think she's taking advantage of it, though."

Their food arrived and they dug in. Bonnie was away visiting her sister in Denver, Kent told Jay, making the most of her much needed holiday. The door to Lots banged shut.

Jay looked up, and seeing Gordie Lonker, told his brother the baron wannabe was in their presence. He hadn't bothered to lower his voice. Kent grinned and kept eating. Gordie came to stand beside their table, immediately angry.

"I got the special permit, did you hear?"

"No, Gordie, I didn't," Jay sighed. "And I can't say I'm glad, either."

"I can't either," Kent joined in.

"No," Gordie answered shortly, "I didn't suppose either of you would be. After your organizing those protesters at the county board meeting, I'm surprised that's all you have to say."

Jay slowly wiped his mouth and moved his chair back from the table. Nearby diners looked up from their meals and watched. It was no secret that Gordie and the Robbins men didn't see eye to eye.

"I don't like your leasing out your property for that big feed lot," Jay began. "And I'm not going to sit here and hide the way I feel about it from you or anyone else. If that's how you want to make your money, that's your business. It's my business to say I don't want it in my neighborhood."

"Your neighborhood?" Gordie was irate. "My land is two miles the other side of town. I'm nowhere near where either of you live!" His face was brick red. "Where the hell do you get off tell-

ing me what I can and can't do? You don't control all the land around here, even if your
granddaddy did help settle this part of the country." He sneered this.

"That's not the point, Gordie," Jay sighed.
He looked at his brother and Kent shook his
head, reaching for another roll. "The point is,"
Jay continued, straining for patience, "you're the
one leasing land to the feed lot. And that's going
to benefit just one person, and it won't even be
you." Gordie began sputtering.

"I've got nothing at all against feed lots," Jay
said. "Feed lot or any other kind of business
aren't negatives as far as I'm concerned. But the
positive benefits of the incoming business sure
as hell better outweigh the negatives. The size
and location of this one is just begging problems. You'll get some money and we'll all get the
headaches. If they were smaller, or located further away or in a different direction from
town..." Jay said. "There are all kinds of ways it
could work, if you and they wanted it to work.
But that's the problem, isn't it?"Jay swished
around the water in his glass. His voice was dead
calm. "They won't buy much locally and when
they see a better deal somewhere else they'll pull
out and leave you with a cesspool of problems,
foremost of which is that everyone here will hate
your guts for bringing that mess here in the first
place. Feed lot or manufacturer or most any
other big deal operation— anything that large,
that concentrated, or located that close to civilization with that much large scale environmental

fallout and no workable plan to address it—is a bad deal for everyone."

He took a drink and set down his glass. "It's factory farming and you know it. And I know you don't give a shit. I say you're wrong and I'm sorry as hell the county board didn't have the guts to stop you."

Kent offered Jay a dinner roll and nodded toward the butter. Jay shook his head and finished. "I don't want to argue with you, Gordie. You and I haven't ever really gotten along and I can accept that. I know I have no legal way of stopping you from doing what you're bound and determined to do. The point that this will hurt people, and won't exactly be good for the environment around here is one you don't see. That's fine. Just don't stick it in my face and expect me to condone it, let alone congratulate you for it."

He stood up and reached for the bill, Kent following him to the counter where they both paid for their meals and walked out, leaving Gordie in the wake of their departure.

ℰᎠℭᎡ

By Saturday afternoon everyone on the west wing of the State House was ready to go home and forget about rural development and the Ag crisis. They had put in a week and then some.

Liz didn't really boss. She made suggestions, challenged, asked for assistance, checked on progress, and assigned tasks. In a word she was a leader. One who didn't rest until it was done right so how could those around her rest?

Now they were all exhausted and ready for a break, both from the work and from one another.

During the drive home she critiqued her week. For the most part she was satisfied. There was a feeling, deep inside, that not enough had been accomplished, but it would have to do. She was home now.

When she drove through Benton she could feel herself shifting into a different gear, shedding the tensions of the meetings and calls and dozens of deals. She had called Annie when she left Kearney so her kids would be ready when she arrived.

It's beautiful, she thought with surprise, as she pulled into Pearse. She was beginning to really see the winter season. The grasses took on such a surprising variance in their muted colors. God, how she had come to love this part of the world.

Jane rushed from Roger and Annie's house, grabbing her mom before she was fully out of the car. Liz hugged her tightly, reveling in the feel of those young arms grasping her.

Then she reached behind Jane for Tess and Ben. Annie came out of the house with three bags and loaded them in the trunk. "They were great. Thanks for letting us keep them," she told Liz, ruffling Ben's hair and hugging each of them goodbye. Liz thanked Annie for everything and drove to the Red Door.

That night they played board games and caught up on their week apart.

13

Kent told Liz after church the next morning that his brother had flown to Albuquerque Saturday. "It kind of came up fast," Kent said, grinning fully. "Something about having an important meeting in Lincoln Tuesday," Kent went on. "Know anything about that?"

"Well, there's a press conference Tuesday morning," she hedged. They asked how her week in Lincoln went and Liz told them what her part in the initiative was and what else she still needed to do.

She took her kids home. In between feeding loads of clothes into the washing machine and dryer, she spent the afternoon outside with Ben and the girls.

After packing her bag for her last trip to Lincoln, Liz made out a list of her goals for the next two days. Then she checked to make sure the kids' bags were ready and by the door.

Tomorrow they would take the bags aboard the bus and put them in Annie's car once they arrived at school. Bonnie had agreed to call in the morning to make sure they got up in time to eat breakfast. Annie and Roger were again going to care for the Daniels kids while their mom was gone.

Liz left at 4:30 in the morning, arriving at the State House at 7:15. She went to Behlend's office and invited Angie and Jim to join her for coffee.

Jim and Angie made small talk about their respective weekends. Then Liz glanced at her notepad and began to outline what needed to be done that day and the next.

"I was home this weekend, too," she said when she had finished. She smiled at both of them as she smoothed out the lines of her skirt and sipped from her mug. "It was great. The kids and I had a wonderful time together. I got outside, did a little hiking, saw some of the new baby calves in my neighborhood. I feel restored."

She looked at them sharply now. "I've got to warn you, if you thought I was bad last week, I'm going to be hell on wheels this week." Jim was surprised into laughter. Angie choked on her coffee, looking at Liz to see if she was kidding. She was not.

Liz wanted all of them focused on their objective. "I know that what is happening in rural America is not unique, what with all the consolidations and buyouts and large businesses left after the dust settles. It's happening with all industries, everywhere. But I don't like it. I don't believe it's positive for this country." She walked to her desk, turned on the monitor, and sat down to switch on her computer.

Liz swivelled back to them and chuckled without humor. "It's really kind of funny when you think about it. When an inner city neighborhood says it's going to take a stand against crime and drug dealing and vows 'not in my neighborhood,' we respect that. We know they can't possibly get rid of all crime or all drug dealers, but we believe they can shove them out of their neighborhood."

She flicked on her printer. Angie rolled toward the doorway, Jim walking with her. The three looked at one another. Liz continued. "Why doesn't Nebraska take a stand against the loss of family farms and ranches and say 'not in my state'? We could, you know. We're going to, tomorrow morning, ten o'clock sharp." She turned to her desk and picked up the phone.

ഇരുള

Liz finished putting on her make-up. She eyed herself critically in the mirror and nodded. She was ready for the press conference.

She wasn't officially taking part in it. She had, however, planned everyone's role. Jim Behlend would welcome everyone, outlining why the rural initiative was vitally important and why the governor had decided to step it up.

Then he would call Governor Moreland up to the podium. Members of the advisory group from around the state would come up behind the governor to listen to his words of wisdom.

Liz had orchestrated everything down to who would stand directly behind the governor. The photos in the newspapers and bites on television would show some of the most respected and powerful people in the state standing unified behind him.

Following the governor's announcement and outline of his new plan, he would open up the press conference to questions, something he almost never did.

He had argued long and fiercely with Liz about this point but she had argued back, yelling only slightly lower than he out of deference to his position. In the end, she'd won. She promised to prep him for the questions and had spent an hour last night doing so.

As a precaution, she'd prepared Jim Behlend as well. Liz had scheduled the governor for only a few minutes of questions and answers and then Behlend would move in to wind up the session, indicating to the press that he would personally oversee the governor's views in carrying out the rural initiative.

Governor Moreland was privately very pleased with everything she'd done. Outside of the circle of Jim and Angie, however, he said nothing. He needed to score voter points and he intended to glean all the credit he could from the efforts of the past eight days.

Pete and Sandra kicked the project into a second high gear. Liz decided that by Monday night they had accomplished what she'd wanted of them and sent them back to Minneapolis. The governor had finally boiled over once he found out about that. "I paid how much to bring two people here for how many hours!"

Now as she stood waiting for the press conference to begin she remembered the success of the first advisory meeting late the evening before and smiled to herself at the governor's opening comment to the group.

When he referred to his decision to bring in a team of experts from Minneapolis to put the final touches on his initiative, Liz had coughed into her hand. It was one of her cardinal rules, after all: Be tactful at all times, and never laugh when such an action would be inappropriate.

Liz saw that the television stations had their lights and cameras set up and their microphones in hand. The radio and print media were assembled and ready. She signaled to Jim and to the sound crew, then leaned against the wall off to the side, watching the carefully choreographed show unfold.

Following Jim and the governor, she listened to the question and answer period and watched as the press ran for the doorways, anxious to make deadline with the story of the week on both the campaign and the farm crisis front.

As Liz was shaking hands with the governor and Jim, Angie handed her a note and a box. "Someone handed them to me and said I was to give them to you after the press conference. He's right..." she said, looking toward the back of the room. "Now where did he go?"

Liz took them and saw the handwriting on the envelope. Jay's, she thought, and she looked for him as she and Angie crossed the lawn to the governor's Mansion for the reception. Liz received congratulations from several of the advisory members and a bear hug from Jim. A few minutes later she found a quiet corner, away from the growing crowd, to read the short message.

Liz,

I'm done waiting for you. No more promises about space and time.

And I won't take no. Marry me. We'll make a home for the five of us and whatever happens, we'll deal with it, together.

Love,
Jay

She looked up and saw him standing beside Jim and Angie, watching her as he chatted with them, that damn grin of his in place. Oh, Lord, Liz.

Then she opened the box. Inside was an antique diamond ring. Liz didn't think. She didn't need to. For weeks she'd been trying to analyze something that in her heart she'd already known. He was good for her, they were right for one another. She took the ring out of the box and put it on her left ring finger.

Liz heard Jay shout even before she saw him striding over to her. He tugged her further back into the corner of the room. "I would pick you up in the air, darlin', but I know you don't like the public thing."

She looked at all the people in the room, many whose arms she'd severely twisted to ensure their attendance. "Sometimes, Jay, you've got to forget about everyone out there and just worry about those in your circle."

She smiled, and taking his face in her hands, kissed him. "I've got to do some things now," she said reluctantly pulling away, "and I don't have any pockets so you'll have to hold onto these for me." She handed him the box and note.

Walking over to the governor, she began working him around the room, dealing his way into a second term as Governor of the great state of Nebraska.

೫ CR

Annie and Roger toasted their friends. The prenuptial practice at St. Mary's was followed by a dinner at their home in Pearse. All of Liz's family was there as was Jay's. Ruby had declined, saying she wanted to rest up for the following day.

Liz's sisters had loved Jay from the moment they'd met. Their husbands and the Robbins brothers had hit it off immediately and were now engaged in a conversation ranging from Husker football to the economy and the presidency.

At ten o'clock Liz suggested an end to the evening. Raymond and Anita were quick to agree and drove off to the Red Door.

As Liz thanked Annie and Roger, she noticed her sisters and their husbands deep in conversation with Kent and Lisa's husband Dave, as they moved outdoors. When their eyes moved toward her, she knew it was payback time. Her sister Megan was the first to speak. "Liz. We've been visiting."

"Megan, wonderful sister of mine, I am truly ashamed of the little things I may have assisted in doing to you and Paul on your wedding day. And Teresa, fabulous sister of mine, ditto for you and Frank."

"Sorry Lizzy," Teresa spoke up, "your last minute apologies won't save you from a few drinks at the local bar which Jay assures us is known as the best Bloody Mary place in the region. And just where do you get off with this 'assisted' stuff? You were the ring leader."

Her sisters arranged themselves on each side of Liz. "I distinctly remember Frank warning you," Teresa said, "that you would suffer the consequences of your actions and you just laughed at him, like it would never catch up. Well, Liz," Teresa said pointedly, "your time has come."

Jay joined in. "She had me believe she was an innocent. Are you telling me at my eleventh hour that she's not who I thought she was?" They entered Bubbles Bar on the street corner across from the bank.

Kent challenged Jay to remember half of what he'd pulled at wedding receptions.

"Sounds like the two of you are going to have a big day tomorrow," Megan commented dryly.

Jay ordered a round, then walked over to the pool table where he and Liz invited her sisters to a game. Lisa and Bonnie entertained the rest with stories of Kent and Jay's escapades in and out of school.

Later that night, they stood outside as their vehicles warmed. "No wonder you like it out here. What a peaceful, quiet part of the world you live in." Teresa, from upstate New York, was enthralled with Pearse.

"Frank," she said to her husband, "wouldn't it be great to live where our children could walk home from school and play ball in the neighborhood park without us constantly hovering over them?"

"Remember," Liz cautioned, "this may not be Minneapolis or Ithaca, but there are crazies everywhere. The sheriff and police departments keep pretty busy."

"But how wonderful" Megan said, "that our two children could play outside in our yard while I walked down to the corner. We just don't do that. Teresa, didn't you tell me about friends of yours who weren't allowed to play in their yards when they were kids?"

"There's a trade off in living here," Jay explained. "Some of us are able to move back here because we understand how these little towns operate, and because we had careers that could move here. But it doesn't work that way for a lot of people in the rural areas. A lot of jobs pay lousy—many below minimum wage—and benefits, if there are any, are usually pretty paltry."

They were now gathered near the curb. "The lifestyle can't be beat," Jay said, "if you end up in a can-do community. But the financial reward is sometimes hard to find. I think that's improving

especially with this new entrepreneurial attitude. Thank God for cell phones and e-mail. But I
still think it can be really tough to move in when
you don't have any connections, any relationships already built here. Just ask Liz about learning the ways of Benton."

She smiled in answer. "But the trade off is
like that phrase goes, 'the whole village is raising
my family'. I know it's going to take me a long
time to understand Benton. But with every job
I've ever had I went through a similar learning
curve. If the community gives you just half a
chance, it can work out. I do think the more people who move into these small towns and the
more diverse their opinions, the more accepting
Bentonites will become."

She hugged her sisters goodnight. Lisa and
Dave drove back to Kearney. Jay and Liz stepped
into the back of Kent and Bonnie's Suburban
while Megan and Paul, and Frank and Teresa followed in their rental car back to Benton and to
their motel. Dropping Jay off at Liz's place, the
Suburban continued on up the road.

After starting his pickup, Jay walked Liz to
her porch, glancing up at the sound of an air-
plane on its trek from Omaha to Denver.

"Well, I suppose I'd better get in and see if
everyone found a place to sleep," she said in an
exhausted voice.

"Are all the kids here tonight?" Jay asked.

"They are," she nodded. "I told my sisters to
just leave them and drive out after breakfast to
get them. That way we don't have to wake anyone tonight or take them out in the cold. Mom

and Dad came home and relieved the babysitter."

Jay tipped Liz's chin upward. "So what time are we to be at the church tomorrow for pictures? Around noon?"

"At noon. Straight up. The photographer said she can get our shots in about half an hour and that gives us a few minutes before the early arrivals."

They kissed tenderly. "Just one thing for you to think about while we're going through all the rigamarole tomorrow," Jay said as he walked down the steps to his truck.

Liz barely concealed a yawn. "What?"

He was standing next to his truck now. "As far as I'm concerned tomorrow is just another day and it's also a big day. A big day because I get to be with you from here on out. And I get to stand up in front of God and everybody and make promises to you that I'm going to keep."

"Oh, Jay, if you're not careful I'm going to start crying and I'm going to look like I partied too heartily tonight." She could feel her chest moving in and out in a dizzy kind of way, like when she watched a good movie and a scene was just too emotional.

Jay smiled as he opened his door, the pickup now warm from the few minutes the engine had run. He looked at Liz standing near her porch door. "And just another day because ever since I met you, Liz, since the first time in Lots when you were pretty put out with me, I've wanted to marry you. I may not have recognized it right away, but that's a fact."

He stepped into the cab and leaned out his window to finish. "So tomorrow's just one more day. Being in the church and everyone dressing up nice is great. The prayers and the sacrament are good things. I'm sure we're going to have a ball at the party afterwards. But I don't really need the wedding ceremony to make me feel any more committed, any more connected to you than I do right now. I love you Elizabeth Ann Klinsky Daniels. See you at the church at noon. Straight up."

Jay drove back to town.

She had to rinse her eyes in ice water for five minutes.

By the time her sisters had arrived the next morning, Liz and her parents had fed all of the kids and cleaned up the kitchen. Liz slipped away for a quick walk, dressed in layers and striking out into the pasture as she did most mornings.

Drifts, cold, wind—all of this she relished. The harder she had to push, the more she enjoyed it. Normally she'd dissect problems, conjure up creative ideas, or hold imaginary conversations to work through whatever was bothering her.

But this was her wedding day. This morning's hike was for pure enjoyment. She left her mind free to simply look forward to the day. She was cresting the hill above the barn on her return when she saw Jay drive in and walk up the steps of the porch.

A few minutes later she saw him coming out of the house and, shading his face with his hand, look in her direction. He leaned against the pickup, waiting. She was breathing hard from the effects of good exercise when she drew near him.

"Morning ma'am." They kissed and she backed away, lifting her arms above her head to force air back into her lungs.

"Don't you know you're supposed to stay away from the bride on the morning of your wedding?" Liz said when she could talk.

Jay laughed, "I've heard that before, but I don't pay attention to that sort of thing. How was your walk?"

"Invigorating. It took a little longer than I'd planned, though, so I'd better get in the house and get ready. What's up?"

"We've never really talked about our honeymoon," he answered. "I guess we were just going to play it by ear and that's still fine with me, but..."

Liz arched her eyebrow. "Oh, oh. Here it comes."

He walked with her to the foot of the steps. "We've been given a trip for two to Angel Fire, New Mexico. John Daly and his wife can't go. Their youngest son's wife suddenly needs some pretty serious surgery and they're going to Lincoln to help take care of their grandkids. He called this morning and offered the trip to us if we're interested. Airline tickets, motel, lift passes, the works. Plane takes off from Kearney tonight at nine o'clock."

"Sounds wonderful."

"That's what I thought. I told him to bring them. They were planning on coming to the wedding and then heading off to Lincoln afterward. Ever been to Santa Fe?"

"I've never been to New Mexico," she said.

"You're going to love it." He backed away toward his truck. "See you at noon."

14

Waiting at the entrance to the church with Jay were his attendants Roger and Kent and his friend Steve from Kansas City. Liz's sisters, their husbands and children soon arrived.

Shortly afterwards the organist and vocalist entered and went to the front of the church to go over a piece of music one last time. Dave and Lisa came with their two, followed by Bonnie and her kids. Both ushers came in together and held the door for Liz as she arrived with her parents and children and Annie.

Liz's silk floor length cream colored dress was cut simply, the skirt falling in tiny pleats and long sleeves with small lace edging above her fingertips. She wore only the pearl earrings given her by her matron of honor, her mother's pearl necklace, and Jay's ring.

The wedding took on a life of its own, everyone playing a role as if in a production directed and produced by someone other than themselves. The photographer and florist arrived. Bouquets and boutonnieres were dispensed.

Photos began and music practice ended. Children ordered to stop squirming, camera flashes flashing. Groupings made and made again. Priest talking with the altar servers. Mother of bride teary, then fine.

More pictures and laughter. People enjoying themselves in anticipation. Liz and Jay simply part of the life of this wedding, not really in charge anymore, swept up in the movement forward toward that time at the front of the church when they would be joined.

Children fascinated by it all. Photos completed. Wedding party and families moving to adjacent classrooms to adjust hair, check make-up, straighten tousled jackets and double-knot little shoes.

After twelve-thirty, people arriving. Ruby resting in back pew. Friends and relatives seated, beginning their role of supporters for this couple and their embarkment. Candles lit, soft clavinova music played. Five minutes 'til one.

Ruby ushered to second pew. Anita and Raymond ushered forward. Jane and Ben and Tess with them. Teresa and Megan's children next with their dads. Bonnie and her three kids placed next to Ruby. Lisa and Dave's family seated.

Father Bob now coming from the side door, stepping forward, greeting all, announcing purpose of gathering this day. Megan and Steve coming up aisle to Bach's "Jess Joy of Man's Desiring." Next Teresa and Kent.

In Benton

Slowly, majestically. Altar servers standing beside Father Bob. Anita and Raymond relaxing in the good will of this day. Ben, having trouble swallowing, seeing mom in the back of the church, ready to come up the aisle with Jay. Jane enthralled by the romance, the beauty of it all. Tess, tired of her new shoes.

Roger and Annie, slowly stepping up the aisle. Music building. Liz watching the people she loves. Jay seeing childhood friends, relatives. Liz and Jay, both ready for this moment, their hands clasped.

Annie and Roger reach the altar, part to their respective sides. Priest steps forward. Altar servers step forward. People lean forward, stand. Music fading.

Now it is Jay and Liz whom everyone focuses on. Liz grips her white roses. Pachabel's "Canon in D" begins.

And then, once again, they are in charge of their wedding day. Time ends its surreal dance and they walk up the aisle.

They pledged themselves to one another. Following the readings they'd selected, Father Bob gave a tough love sermon sprinkled with humor.

They exchanged rings. Their families shared the sign of peace with them. The Ave Maria was sung acappella. They shared in the communion and two lines of guests came forward from the pews to do the same.

The final reading. The final blessing. And finally Father Bob's announcement: "Would you please join me in congratulating Liz and Jay Robbins."

Applause filled the church. Ruby and Anita hugged, laughing at the others' tears. The newly weds kissed and left the altar, walking down the aisle as "Craon's Marche Nuptiale no.2" majestically ushered them out.

The photographer nearly missed the shot. The clavinova piece ended and soft service music began.

Liz took Jay's hand and together they walked to the front of the church once more, this time to greet their guests one at a time as they left and made their way to the reception. Pew after pew was emptied to the accompaniment of hugs and kisses, laughter, and smiles.

They talked to the last person in the last seat and then stood a minute, enjoying the final notes of the last wedding song. Thanking the organist and vocalist, their ushers, family, and their attendants, Jay and Liz stepped out into the sunshine. And were instantly bombarded with bird seed.

"I forgot about the rice thing." Liz gasped as Jay tried to cover her, seed raining all around them.

"Me too," Jay said. "And I used to shovel it out pretty good. Liz," an apology in his eyes, "I think from now until we leave town tonight we're really going to pay for my sins." They survived the last handfuls and moved next door to the party.

Ben walked up to them, shyly congratulating them. Liz bent to kiss his cheek and Jay gave him a hug. A small dance band began playing. Several guests had already found their way to the bar. Roger brought them two glasses of wine. "Welcome to the club," he said in salute. They took a sip.

"Hold these again, would you Roger?" Liz asked. She turned to Jay and took both his hands. "If we cut the cake right away, our hosting responsibilities are finished."

"Let's cut the cake, Mrs. Robbins." They posed for a picture in front of the wedding cake and went through the buffet, sitting at a table near the dance floor. The wedding party and all of their families followed them through the buffet line and seated themselves around the hall.

Roger and Kent both made toasts. Teresa toasted on behalf of the Klinsky family. "For the past couple of days, I've been trying to figure out," Annie said when her turn was next, "what I wanted to say to you, Liz and Jay. I decided to thank you two for showing all of us how to live."

Liz frowned, waiting for her to explain. "Remember, my friend, when you first moved here and we were talking about what you were going to do in Benton? Remember? You said you just wanted to dig in the dirt, take care of your kids, and no more impossible relationships? Well, I may have only been married a short while, but let me assure you that what you are undertaking is pretty well impossible! Good luck!"

The crowd roared and then someone did it. Someone picked up a fork and started tapping on a water glass. Others followed suit and soon the whole room was calling for a kiss. Having seen this at Annie and Roger's wedding, Liz wasn't entirely surprised.

With great enthusiasm Jay took her in his arms and leaned her backward, kissing her breathless. Sitting down again amidst the whistles and cheers, he asked Annie what she meant by her impossible relationship and good luck comments.

"As much as I know of you and what I'm learning about marriage," Annie laughed, "she's going to need all the luck she can muster. What on earth could be easy about two people coming together? Yet here we all are." With that, Roger claimed Annie for a dance.

Still laughing from Annie's comments, Jay held Liz close, and the band moved into a waltz. Heads lifted around the room to watch the new couple.

"I suppose she's right." Jay turned his head toward Liz's face as she continued. "If I really wanted my life to be easy, uncomplicated, I'd have stayed away from you."

"Why darlin', look at all the fun you'd have missed. Say, do you think you still have seed in there somewhere?" His eyes ogled her teasingly.

Smiling innocently she answered, "I'm sure I do and I'm also sure you're not going looking, at least not right now." They smiled at one another.

Annie cut in and asked Jay to dance, Roger taking Liz's hand. Then she danced with her dad while Jay danced with Anita. People ate and drank and told stories. John Daly and his wife handed over their tickets and wished them a good trip.

By five most people had left for home, and Liz's sisters and their families went to their motel rooms to rest. Kent and Bonnie's family had left to do a few winter evening chores, and Ruby was relaxing at home, waiting for her weekly phone call from Annie's parents.

Anita and Raymond took Liz's car and drove their grandchildren out to the Red Door. Roger and Annie dropped off the new couple at a garage on the far side of town where Jay had hidden his pickup that morning.

Having shivareed more than a few friends, he'd decided the best course was to hide his vehicle. The Wallrons drove off honking.

Suspecting, but not believing, Jay opened the garage door and discovered the depths to which his best man would go. Liz stood shivering while Jay stared at the truck, then climbed in and backed it out between the narrow doors.

He quickly opened his door and taking Liz by her waist lifted her up, wrapping his arms around her as they waited for the truck to warm.

"I go to the trouble of finding a place for the truck so it won't get soaped all over, I don't say a word to anyone, and Rog finds it anyway! How'd he do it?"

"Annie promised me the look on your face would be worth the trouble it took to clean it. All I said was no soap, no tape. I love the cowboy boots tied to the back bumper. Nice touch." Then she smiled innocently.

Jay stared at her, amusement there along with disbelief. "You told them where I hid it?"

"I couldn't help myself," she admitted. "I remembered your last birthday and helping hide you. And that time at the Thanksgiving dance when you ordered up the solo for Roger and Annie. When Kent and Roger asked," she lifted her shoulders, "I told." They sat a few minutes longer, talking in tender, soft tones. Then they drove home to the Red Door.

The goodbyes took a bit. Liz hadn't been away from her children very often since moving to Benton. Stopping at Jay's house to pick up his luggage, they drove under the evening stars to the airport in Kearney, watching for deer along tree-lined creeks.

They flew first to Denver, then to Albuquerque, where they reserved a car before checking in at the airport motel.

"The Dalys made wonderful travel plans," Liz murmured as she lay in the arms of her husband later that night. "I'll have to remember to call them the next time we want to go somewhere."

Jay kissed her hair gently.

"Hmm, you seem pretty content," she commented.

"I keep thinking it can't get any better and then it happens," he answered softly. "I'm not naive. I know that you and I, our marriage, won't be perfect. But I'm pretty pleased with my choice, yes."

"Your choice, is it?" She rolled out of his arms and onto her elbows on his chest, looking full into his face. "And I didn't play a role here?"

He pulled her back down beside him, kissing her forehead, then her cheek, then lingering on her lips. "Well, let's just say you were a little slow when we first met but you're doing mighty fine now."

They slept a few hours, rising early to pick up their rental car and to drive before sunrise to Santa Fe. Jay remembered a restaurant where he'd eaten many good breakfasts so they parked in the Plaza area and dined at La Fonda. Their waiter's service was impeccable.

During the course of their meal they visited with him about Santa Fe. As Liz handed Jay his credit card from the man's tray, she asked the waiter to recommend a good Mass service.

"San Miguel. It is very beautiful, and I think you will enjoy her music. Five tonight, Senora." They spent the day wandering around the small city, studying its architecture, surveying the shops and galleries.

They made mental notes of places they planned to visit later in the week. Shortly before five they arrived at San Miguel and found room toward the center of the church. Kneeling side by side, they shared in this southwestern style of worship. The music was vibrant, full of life.

Monday was spent exploring Taos in much the same way. The galleries and studios were wonderful. They picked up a painting, a few small prints, and a sand painting, arranging to have their purchases shipped home.

Liz was driving back to their motel above Santa Fe at dusk when she pulled their car to the side of the road and looked out over the scenic mountains and canyons during another beautiful New Mexico sunset.

She glanced at Jay, "I don't think we could have come up with a better place to honeymoon than this. Is this a coincidence or is something at work here?"

"I don't know," Jay nodded to his right, "but that view over there is something else, isn't it?"

They sat silently and watched the sun slip away, shadows at play, the jagged lines of terrain becoming softer until only a hint of the smudged images remained.

"Reminds me of my life." Liz said it so quietly Jay wasn't sure she'd spoken.

He turned his head, meeting her gaze. "Why?"

"Because sometimes when things seem really dark, good things manage to slip through." She reached for his hand, feeling his strength.

"I would have sworn a year ago that moving to Benton was a pretty stupid choice. But not all of my so-called 'intelligent' decisions in life turned out too hot so why not just leap and have a little faith that it will all work out somehow, right?"

She drew in a sharp breath. "I didn't want to see you, date you, come to care for you. I wanted everything safe and simple and quiet. Well, that didn't work so great either. And where am I now?" She leaned over to kiss him, then turned on the ignition and drove the last few miles to their motel below the amphitheater.

Tuesday and Wednesday they spent skiing Angel Fire east of Taos. The following two days they explored Santa Fe more thoroughly. They bought jewelry from different craftsmen and women, toured a pueblo, and saw the miraculous staircase in the Loretto Chapel. They wandered in and out of stores and shops, stopping in at this small museum or art gallery, that small furrier or jeweler.

Evenings they sought out good restaurants and later, after making love, fell asleep in each other's arms, sheets tangled around them. Mornings they talked and talked, rising early to eat and share the day together. By Saturday they were ready to be home. They arrived at the airport in Kearney about an hour after dark and were waiting for their luggage when someone tapped Liz on the shoulder.

She turned and looked directly into her brother-in-law's face. "Kent! What are you doing here?"

Jay walked over carrying two bags. "Hey, big brother. What brings you to the airport?"

"Bonnie and I and Lisa and Dave thought we'd meet you two and go out for supper. It may be the last time we all get away without the kids for awhile so we thought we'd surprise you." They each took a piece of luggage and walked out to the parking lot where the rest of the family waited in the Robbins Suburban.

80CR

Annie had called a couple nights earlier inviting them out to Lots to celebrate Liz's thirty-fifth birthday. She was just pulling on her favorite pair of jeans when Jay walked into the bedroom to see if she was ready to go.

"Hmm, I must have gained a little weight."

"None that I can detect," his eyes keenly interested.

Her temperature spiked. "When you look at me like that, I feel like a teenager."

"Darlin', you still look like a teenager. God I love you!" He pulled her to him. "And I'm going to have this look in my eye for a long, long time."

Someone knocked on their bedroom door. Ben stuck his head in. "Mom? Jay? Do I have to make sandwiches for the girls? They're old enough to do it themselves and Lea Ann shouldn't have to do it either. I don't even know why we need a babysitter."

"I agree," Jay said. "You guys don't really need anyone here to do anything for you. It's more of a precaution in case something major should go wrong." He thought a second, looked at Liz for agreement.

"Tell you what," she said. "We get a good report from Lea Ann about homework, getting along, bed times, and we'll have a talk about no more sitter in the future..."

Ben's silent cheer was interrupted by Jay's words "...under certain circumstances."

"Jay?"

"Yeah?"

"You're really catching on fast to this parent thing."

"I'll take that as a compliment," Jay chuckled, ruffling Ben's hair. Then he looked back at Liz, "Ready?"

She nodded quickly. "I'll be out in a minute."

Jay and Ben walked out together, Jay opening the porch door for Lea Ann who had just arrived. Then he stepped outside to admire the green sprouting up everywhere.

"The birds are going wild, aren't they?" Liz commented as they drove into town.

"They're getting spring fever full throttle," Jay agreed. "Calving's about done. Looks like nature's going to kick in with births all over the place now. Pretty soon we'll see baby pheasant, and then fawns."

Annie and Roger arrived as Jay and Liz were getting out of the pickup. Deciding on their menu choices, Liz found herself steering clear of her favorite items and settling on a tossed salad. "Aren't you hungry tonight, birthday girl?" Annie asked.

"I don't know, I've felt funny all day, like maybe I'm getting the flu. Anyone sick in school?"

"No. But then maybe what you have isn't contagious," Annie said without thinking. And then she looked at her friend's face more closely. "Liz. Are you?"

Roger and Jay turned their attention to their conversation. Liz returned Jay's look.

"Oh, my God. That's why I've felt so funny the past few days!" Heads turned as he took her into his arms and kissed her soundly. "Now wait a minute," she protested, conscious of the looks they were getting. She lowered her voice. "I don't know for sure."

Annie dryly retorted, "You're the mom of three. I bet you know what pregnant feels like." Liz was adjusting to the thoughts streaking through her brain and didn't notice Jay's face. Annie later told her she wished she'd had a video camera along. "You two were a riot."

Liz stayed with her salad choice. During their meal Jay noticed her staring out the window toward the pasture grass near town. "It's not as tall as it was a year ago, is it?"

She turned to him and smiled. The cupcake and candle sent out from the kitchen topped off a good celebration. Annie got Liz to promise to share the news the second they knew for certain.

Jay didn't drive home. Instead he headed west of town to some pasture land his family had owned for years. It was rougher country than where they lived. With breaks and steep canyons, wildlife habitat everywhere, it immediately appealed to Liz for the utter privacy it afforded.

He parked near a stand of trees and got out. Opening her door he led her to old logs drug into some semblance of a square shape. He waited for her to sit. "How do you feel?"

"Oh, kind of full, a little queasy. Everything in my body feels like it's anticipating something, like it's getting ready for something. It's really similar to the flu except I've felt this before and it wasn't the flu."

She watched him kick his boot in the sand, making a mark on the ground, then look up at her with wonder on his face.

"I hope you're happy with this because I have to tell you I'm thrilled. Beyond thrilled. I feel a little guilty, though, because of Ben and Jane and Tessy."

"Guilty?"

"I love them," he said. "But this is different."

"Oh, that," she nodded, understanding. "Honey, the first time you're expecting is so special. All babies are, but the first time is such a wonder. You're anticipating all the promise this world holds. Ben was that way for me. And this one will be because it's yours and mine. So don't feel guilty. If I am really pregnant, and I'm pretty sure I am, just enjoy yourself. I'm going to."

"You're okay with this?"

"For heaven's sake, Jay," she laughed, "I did know what we were doing," and then more seriously, "Yes, I'm very okay with this. I suppose I had even hoped it would be sooner rather than later and it looks like that's how it's going to turn out. I told you as far as I was concerned marriage and family go hand in hand. That's just how I am."

He relaxed for the first time since Annie and Liz had stumbled onto the subject.

"Why here to talk?" she asked, walking to the large log on the opposite side.

"This is where I was going to build my cabin for my wife and family." She spun around. "I always thought that I would build my own home for my wife and our beautiful children. When I was a little kid I just did the Davy Crockett thing here but when I was in high school I imagined living here with that view." He put his hand up and drew it across the horizon. Liz turned to look again.

"I planned to live here and teach my kids to love the rural way of life as much as I did." He walked to her, holding her from behind, his hands spread gently across her stomach.

"I'm not ranching because it's too damn tough and too disappointing for me. And I love architecture and building. Always did. But I can still show our kids how to love and respect this kind of place. I guess what I'm saying is I am thrilled about a baby and I want to build a house here for all of us. You need more office space and so do I. The house in town is great but won't work for all of us either. And we're going to need more room again in about, what, eight and a half months or so?"

He looked into the distance and went on, "How would you feel about a log home right around here? We're still only about a mile and a half from town and right off the highway so roads in bad weather won't be an issue. The view in every direction is worth a million bucks and Kent and Lisa and I wouldn't sell it for ten times that amount. What do you think?"

"I'll have to think about this new house thing but what you've said sounds wonderful. Promise me something? Don't say anything to the kids about the baby for a while. I asked Annie to keep a lid on it, too. I need a little time to adjust, to mentally prepare."

"If I can keep it quiet, I will. But you may be asking something I'm not capable of doing." He twirled her around, lifting her into his arms, and carrying her over to the pickup.

"Hope you're watching where you and the kids go walking these days," he warned. "It's time for the rattlesnakes to be out again."

She glanced down sharply at his feet. "Now you tell me, after we go sludging through the grass."

œ&cre;

Liz had never had full fledged morning sickness before. Early rising, lining up her care giver, and rushing to work had been the story of her pregnancies. This time was different.

She was sick. Miserably, totally, disgustingly sick. And at the same time vibrantly alive. Jay went with her to the clinic appointment two weeks later. She warned him that this alone would cause the news to flash across the valley.

"I'm not the one who wants to keep it quiet," he reminded her.

Mary Sue greeted them as they entered her domain; Jay warmly, Liz with directions to the patient room. Jay followed Liz which effectively took the air out of Mary Sue. The clinic confirmed Liz's internal knowledge.

She was due in January. The P.A. congratulated them and discussed clinic and hospital policies, encouraging them to tour the birthing and delivery rooms ahead of time to become familiar with their set up.

Liz laughed later at the coffee shop. "If history repeats itself, I'll have plenty of time to become familiar with their layout." And then she chuckled at the new father's face. She reached for his hand. "Jay, it's going to be fine."

"I'm just catching on to all of this. It's hard to feel the confidence you feel."

"That's because," she said with certainty, "you're on the outside of the pregnancy and I'm right in there with it. With him or her. You'll settle down when you can feel the baby kick. Then you'll feel more a part of it."

෨෬

It was Liz's birthday. Annie and Roger had just arrived at the Robbins home for a cookout along with their children Jacob and Ellie, now eight and five.

"This is perfect! How did you know I've been wanting his new book?" Liz squeezed Annie's hand and looked over at Bonnie. "You told her, didn't you?"

Nate, now nine, kicked seven-year-old John in the shin who in turn ran to their mother. Liz warned them both to behave and turned back to her next present, this one from Jane.

When the phone rang, Tess ran for the patio door. She came back looking as only a teenager anticipating a boyfriend's call can look when disappointed. She handed the phone to her mother.

Liz laughed at her daughter. "Tess, all the phone calls can't be for you." Liz reached for the phone and said hello.

"Happy Birthday, Mom."

"Ben? Ben, how are you? How are finals going?" Liz stepped into the log home in search of a quiet moment with her long distance eldest.

The Robbins brothers walked toward the edge of the yard, looking across the creek to the pasture spread out before them. "How's it going?" Jay asked.

"Well, I'm pretty well caught up right now with my cattle work," Kent answered, "but if we get all this early warm weather they keep talking about, boy, I don't know."

Jay studied the activity around his home, the party growing noisier as the food got closer to the table. "Remember when we got ol' Vic Moreland back in the governors' office and the whole state got on board the rural initiative deal?"

A deer and its fawn moved across the far side of the pasture, heading toward the west end of the creek. The doe was on lookout for any sign of life, ready to bolt to protect her young.

Jay continued. "You know, that was a pretty big deal. Probably bigger than we realized at the time. I was proud of Liz and the people who stepped up to the plate. And I think we made some inroads. But changing attitudes in people, that was the toughest challenge."

Kent studied his brother. "Don't say it wasn't worth it, Jay. Sometimes it's the effort that counts. Just doing something. Standing for something and be willing to fight for it. I think that's what we did. We stood for something while others sat down. And now that's part of who we are and who they are."

Kent turned back to the house. "Sometimes," he added, "when people laugh at you and tell you you're wrong, that's when you are most right."

Jay nodded solemnly. "Yeah." Then he looked up and grinned. "I like Liz's attitude. What's the point in playing it safe if you're only playing? Hell, it's the living that's the thrill."

About the Author

Raised on a family farm, Mary Ridder works as a freelance news reporter and operates a small public relations firm. She, her husband, and children own a purebred Hereford cattle business in central Nebraska.

Ridder is at work on her second novel.

T0123000078029